Suddenly the air
seemed to shimmer

Blake's features looked distorted. Donna felt the rumble before she heard it and fell to her knees as the ground under her lost its stability and began to shudder and shake to the accompaniment of a sickening, roaring, thundering sound that was everywhere.

A fissure running the full width of the plaza before the temple opened up suddenly, only feet from where she clutched the heaving earth.

She knew she was screaming yet could hear no sound issuing from her lips above the chaos of falling masonry and splitting rock. Both the temple doorway and Blake himself had vanished behind a cloud of dust and debris.

She was entirely alone in a world gone mad!

Books by Kay Thorpe

Harlequin Presents

Harlequin Romances

These books may be available at your local bookseller.

For a free catalog listing all titles currently available,
send your name and address to:

Harlequin Reader Service
2504 West Southern Avenue, Tempe, AZ 85282
Canadian address: Stratford, Ontario N5A 6W2

KAY THORPE

the land of the incas

Harlequin Books

TORONTO • NEW YORK • LONDON
AMSTERDAM • PARIS • SYDNEY • HAMBURG
STOCKHOLM • ATHENS • TOKYO • MILAN

Harlequin Presents first edition November 1983
ISBN 0-373-10646-7

Original hardcover edition published in 1983
by Mills & Boon Limited

CHAPTER ONE

LOOKING down on the vast spread of glittering lights as the plane came in on its final approach, Donna wished she could only turn back the clock on the last three years. When she was twenty this same view of the Peruvian capital had aroused a breathless anticipation she would give a lot to recapture. Inca fever, her father had called it, smiling at her eagerness. It still possessed her, but the feeling was different, the way she was different. Nothing stayed the same; that much she had learned.

Even now, after so many months, she found it hard to reconcile herself to her father's death. They had been so close, especially after she had parted from Blake. Her mind shied away at that point. The last person she wanted to think about right now was Blake. Eventually she was going to have to do something about her marriage, it was true, but for the present she preferred to forget she had a husband and concentrate on the job in hand.

'We're fifteen minutes behind schedule,' observed the fair-haired man in the adjoining seat. 'Not bad, I suppose, considering we were over half an hour late taking off. The house is on the other side of town from the airport. That means a pretty lengthy drive from the look of it down there.'

'See Lima by night,' Donna quipped, turning her head to smile into familiar hazel eyes. 'We'll be there in time for dinner—they eat late out here. How do you feel?'

'Not half as good as you look.' He cast a wry glance over her smooth head of dark gold hair and clear-

5

skinned features. 'No sign of jet-lag about you. I don't know how you do it.'

Blue eyes laughed. 'Mind over matter—plus a little help from comb and lipstick! It's going to be another three or four hours before we can think of turning in, and I need to be fresh when I meet Dr Brinkman for the first time. After all, I'm only here on your recommendation.'

'You're here because you're capable of doing the job you've been hired to do,' came the prompt response. 'Brinkman was more than delighted to have James Campbell's daughter on the team, especially considering your previous experience of this part of the world.'

'I was a rank amateur then,' Donna protested halfheartedly. 'A fine arts graduate and little else. What I've learned about archaeological draughtsmanship since barely qualifies me as a total professional even now. I just hope I can keep my end up, that's all.'

'You will.' It was said with confidence. 'The work you did on your father's last dig is ample proof of that. We're going to make a name for ourselves as a team, you and I.'

Where photography was concerned he already had a name, Donna acknowledged wryly. It was her own ability that still had to be fully proven in the field. Being the daughter of one of the world's finest archaeologists had its drawbacks, in that so much was expected of her. She might well have inherited her father's interests, but she had always known herself incapable of sustaining the years of concentrated study necessary to gaining even a first degree in her own name. The art work had been by way of a compromise. There would always, her father had said, be room for good archaeological draughtsmen. That dig in the Yukon a year ago had been first class field experience, only working for one's own parent had to be a little different from working alongside total strangers, all with far more knowledge to their credit than she could ever hope to muster. On the other hand, Dr Brinkman had apparently been sufficiently impressed with the samples of her work that Graham had sent him to issue the invitation. Why couldn't she just accept that? This expedition was the chance of a lifetime. She owed it both to Graham and to herself to grasp opportunity with both hands, regardless of the whys and wherefores.

Looking out of the port again, she could see a faint reflection of the man at her side as he brought his seat into an upright position in response to the P.A. announcement, rugged features softened by the darkened Perspex. In the six months or so since she had met Graham Horsley they had come to know each other pretty well. Only four years older than herself, he was the most reliable person she had ever known. Just when their relationship had begun to change from simple friendship to something deeper she couldn't exactly say. There had been an empty place in her life and he had begun to fill it, that was as far as she allowed herself to think. Any future they might have together was fraught with problems she was not yet ready to face.

The landing was smooth, the formalities lengthy and tiring. Settled at last in the rear of a cab, Donna put her head back against the rest and gave herself over to contemplation of the coming expedition. In the two years since the discovery of this new 'lost city' there had been only one tentative exploratory mission, and that insufficiently funded to have got very far. With the Linden Foundation behind him, John Brinkman was in a position to spend several months at least delving into the past, with a full and expert team to aid him. Self-doubt touched her mind once more at that point, but she refused to allow it to gain momentum. Confidence was the keynote. While her actual field experience might be limited she was perfectly well aware of what was going to be required of her. Allowing the professional qualifications of others on the team to intimidate her at this stage was no way to get on.

On the surface the city had changed little in the intervening years, the high-rise blocks of the centre giving way to the squalid outer districts where cramped dwellings huddled along the sides of narrow alleys. Their destination lay out in the better-class area towards Miraflores, a large, Spanish-style house set within its own walled gardens. That this had been leased by the foundation as a base at which to bring together the team chosen by Dr Brinkman, Donna already knew. What she had not anticipated was the sheer luxury of the place. It seemed incongruous that from here they were to set out on a trip where creature comforts would be reduced to a minimum.

The incongruity was further enhanced by the uniformed manservant who admitted them to the house via the huge and intricately carved doors. Dinner, he told them in faultless English as he led the way up a wide staircase from the tiled and arched entrance hall, would be served in half an hour.

They had a room each, next door to one another on a long stretch of corridor, both furnished in the same dark wood with a view of the grounds from the window balconies. There was a bathroom opposite, free at present. Donna claimed the privilege of first usage, hastily sorting through her suitcase for clean underwear and one of her two dresses. There had seemed little point in bringing very much formal luggage considering the purpose of the trip. Most of her personal gear consisted of sweaters and slacks to combat the cooler temperatures to be expected in the mountains.

Showered and changed into plain cream linen, she felt

revived enough to regain some of her normal equilibrium. The people gathered in this house shared the same interests and ambitions, and that had to make a good basis. They were part of a team all working towards a unified end. Before tonight was over she would have taken her place among them.

Graham called for her to go downstairs, well-built and attractive in dark slacks and a thin white sweater. Drawn by voices, they moved through one of the archways leading from the hall, to find themselves in a salon of fine proportions and even finer furnishings. Of the six or seven people standing and sitting around the room, only two were female. It was the elder of these, a woman in her early fifties, who made the first move to greet the newcomers, coming to her feet to advance across the floor with a smile etching her finely lined face.

'Hallo, Graham! Can't tell you how good it is to see you again!'

North American, Donna judged, liking the other on sight. Edith Remington, one of America's leading anthropologists, unless she was mistaken. This was a combined venture, with members drawn from both sides of the Atlantic according to John Brinkman's assessment of need. It made her own inclusion even more of a compliment.

Graham confirmed her guess, drawing her forward with a hand on her arm to effect an introduction.

'So you're James Campbell's daughter,' said Dr Remington with a frankly appraising look. 'We worked together on a couple of occasions, your father and I, although not too recently. I was sorry to hear of his death. He was a fine man, and a brilliant archaeologist! Come and meet the rest of the team.'

Names and faces tended to run together during the following moments. Of them all, Donna found herself remembering with clarity only that of the third female in the room. Janine Meade appeared to be no more than in her late twenties, which made her standing in the archaeological world something of a phenomenon by any standards. She looked far from the image Donna had formed of her. Tall and willowy, she wore her ashen hair pulled back in a smooth chignon that emphasised her classic looks. Her eyes were cool.

'I hope we're going to be able to rely on you,' she said. 'Accurate records are essential to any dig.'

'I shan't let you down,' Donna assured her, stifling the urge to say something cutting in return.

'Isn't Dr Brinkman coming down to join us for dinner?' asked Graham into the small silence, moving Donna away with a faint pressure on her arm.

'He didn't get here yet.' It was Edith Remington who supplied the answer, a line appearing between her brows. 'It's odd that we haven't heard anything from him, but he could be coming in on a late flight. If he missed a connection it may even be morning before he arrives.'

'That isn't going to give him much time.'

'Oh, enough. We'll be at least three days at Cuzco acclimatising to the altitude before making tracks for the site. Most of the equipment is being dropped there anyway. I understand we can get to within about thirty kilometres or so of the place by Land Rover, the rest we walk. We'll have llamas as pack animals. There's an Indian village close by.' The anthropologist paused as a gong sounded from the hall. 'There's dinner. I must say, they're doing us proud when it comes to the fine detail. Let's hope we have as good a deal in Cuzco!'

The meal was served by two white-jacketed waiters of mingled Spanish and Indian blood who both spoke Engish in addition to their own language. Conversation among the assembly went on apace throughout, aided not a little by the wine provided in seemingly unlimited quantities. Donna drank sparingly, listening with growing heaviness to the crosstalk in her immediate vicinity, much of which was over her head. These people were without exception of a superior intellect, possessors of limitless knowledge. In that sense, if in no other, she could only feel deficient.

'Bear up,' advised Graham with some understanding before they parted for the night at her door some two hours later. 'If it's any comfort, I'm as far out on a limb as you are when they get stuck into the subject the way they did tonight. Just remember that when it comes to making a good architectural or photographic study we're the specialists.'

His goodnight kiss was terminated with reluctance. Emotional relationships were going to be somewhat limited by conditions these coming weeks. Donna wondered briefly if anyone realised their association was a little more than merely professional. Not that it mattered. They neither of them had any intention of allowing emotion to affect their work in any fashion.

She had been in bed an hour before she finally acknowledged she was not going to sleep without help. There had been a shelf of books down in the salon, she recalled. Perhaps she could manage to read herself into a stupor—always providing she could find something in English, her Spanish being limited. With a cotton wrap pulled on over her sensible pyjama suit, she left the room and made her way downstairs, unsurprised to find lights left burning. In this house expense was obviously no object. She wondered how much it had cost the Foundation to lease the place just for the one night.

There was no one else around that she could see or hear, but the lights in the salon had been switched off. She put on a lamp close by the entrance archway, using its light to make her way across the room to the finely carved bookcase by one of the window embrasures. Spanish *and* English, she was glad to see, viewing the titles. She chose a copy of O. Henry's short stories as the most likely of the collection to provide light reading, finding a moment to wonder idly about the people who owned this house and where they might be at present.

It took the sound of a car coming up the drive outside to jerk her from her thoughts. Dr Brinkman, of course! She got slowly to her feet as the vehicle came to a stop in front of the house, looking down at herself with a faint wry smile. Hardly the ideal dress in which to greet the expedition director for the first time, but neither could she simply ignore the fact that he had arrived and creep away upstairs while he aroused the household for entry. At least this way she would be a step ahead of the others for once.

She found the door locked but not bolted, turning the key to open one half of it before the man outside could get a finger to the bellpush. Shock gripped her by the throat as she gazed at the tall, dark-haired figure standing on the step, widening her eyes in sheer stupefied disbelief. The name came from her lips on a tiny whisper of sound.

'Blake!'

That the shock was not entirely hers was evidenced by the look on the angular face. For a brief moment he seemed turned to stone, eyes almost black in the shadowed moonlight filtering through the trees. His recovery was the swifter of the two, one hand coming out to push the door wider while the other went down to lift the leather bag at his feet.

'I think we'd better discuss this indoors,' he said on a hard note. 'The very last person I expected to find here was *you*!'

Donna backed away a couple of feet as he came in

and closed the door again, barely knowing what to think—or to feel. It was two years since she had last seen this man she had married. How did one cope with a shock of this magnitude?

'I could say the same of you,' she got out, fighting for control over the emotions running riot inside her. 'I thought ... we were expecting Dr Brinkman.'

'Brinkman isn't coming,' he said. 'I'm here in his place.' His lips twisted at the expression that leapt in her eyes. 'Another shock, evidently. I'll be interested to hear just why that piece of news should affect you so badly.'

'What happened to him?' She could scarcely force the words out.

'He had an accident—broke an ankle. Considering the circumstances it was decided to replace him on a temporary basis. He'll be able to take over in a few weeks if the dig proves productive enough to merit an extended stay.' He paused there, studying her with a narrowed intensity that missing nothing of the tumbled golden hair and darkened eyes, the slender curves of her body beneath the thin cotton. 'Which doesn't answer *my* question. What are you doing here, Donna?'

'I'm on the team.' She tried to say it steadily. 'Resident artist for the duration.'

His gaze didn't flicker. 'With what qualifications?'

'I finally took that course at the Institute of Archaeology—including some field work. I also worked with my father on his last dig in the Yukon.' Despite herself she was on the defensive. 'Dr Brinkman thought it enough.'

'Obviously, or you wouldn't be here.' With some deliberation he lowered the leather bag to the floor. 'Is there anywhere I can get a drink? It's been that kind of day.'

'There's a whisky decanter through in the salon,' she said. 'What about food?'

'I'm not hungry.' He started in the direction she had indicated, turning to glance at her when she made no move to follow. 'You'd better come too. This needs talking about.'

She went reluctantly, aware of the necessity yet wary of it too. Standing just within the room, she watched him pour the whisky and toss half of it back in a single swallow before voicing her thoughts.

'Why you?' she asked. 'Of all people, why did it have to be you? Dr Brinkman doesn't even share the same views.'

'The Foundation doesn't take account of personal differences,' he said. 'The grant was made available to John because he was the one to apply. Having got this far with arrangements cancellation was out of the question. I happened to be in a position to make myself available.' He swung to face her, the glass clasped between his fingers. 'Which brings us back to here and now. Sorry as I am to stand in the way of your career, there's no way I'm going to take you along as part of the team.'

'You have to,' she said. 'You don't have any replacement.'

'I'll find one.' Broad shoulders lifted in a gesture which might have been construed as apology, except that Donna knew better. 'Anything else is impossible. You have to see that.'

She saw it with clarity, accepting it was something else again. 'Who's to know about it?' she asked with bitterness. 'Our marriage never made any headlines. I came here under the name of Campbell. Riding on my father's back, I suppose you'd call it.'

'Why not?' He sounded suddenly weary. 'He never accepted you as a Mitchell. The day I stole his beloved daughter away from him was the day I made an enemy for life.'

'He wasn't your enemy. He admired you tremendously! You had so much in common.'

'Professionally we had everything in common. Working with James Campbell was an ambition I'd harboured since finishing university. Marrying you ruined that relationship, only I didn't realise it until it was too late.'

'You mean you wouldn't have asked me to marry you in the first place if you'd realised how my father would take it?'

His shrug came slow. 'Maybe not. Considering how little time it lasted it was hardly a worthwhile exchange.'

'You didn't try very hard to keep me,' she said jerkily. 'Not after . . . the accident.'

There was no change of expression in the grey eyes, only a faint tensing of muscle around his mouth. 'Perhaps there's some truth in that too. Reasons don't really count any more, do they? It's been two years, Donna. Didn't you ever consider asking me for a divorce?'

'Yes,' she admitted. 'Only like you I've tended to let things go. I suppose now would be a good time to thank you for the telegram you sent me when my father died.'

'I hardly imagined my presence would bring you any comfort.' He paused, his regard assessing. 'Was I wrong?'

'No, you weren't wrong.' She was quick to deny the implication—perhaps a little too quick. 'The last person I needed just then was you.'

'Or most other times.' He drained the glass and put it down on the tray behind him, cynicism in the line of his mouth. 'Do you have any idea were I might be sleeping?'

'The room next to mine was to be Dr Brinkman's.'

She hesitated before adding, 'What we were talking about before, it could work if we let it. Is anyone here likely to know about us?'

'That's hardly the point. The situation doesn't lend itself to working conditions. We're all of us going to be living in pretty close confines for some weeks. Tolerance will be at straining point without any added complications.'

'If I can stand it I don't see why you shouldn't,' Donna responded desperately. 'Blake, I need this job!'

Dark brows drew together. 'If you're short of money you only have yourself to blame. You refused to take anything from me.'

'I'm not talking about money. Father left me well enough provided for.' And I want nothing of yours, she almost added, but this was hardly the time. 'It's the prestige; the experience. If I'm thrown off the team now it will be taken as a sign that I'm no good, no matter what kind of excuse you might come up with. Don't do it to me—not for personal reasons.'

'I can't think of better ones.' He shook his head. 'We'll see about getting you on a flight home in the morning. I can have a replacement in Cuzco by evening.'

'I won't go.' Her nails bit into the palm of her hand. 'Not that easily. How would you like it if I told the whole team just why you were so eager to get rid of me? They might consider it less than professional to allow personal problems to influence you, especially at this late date.'

'I daresay I'll bear the strain.' He sounded brusque. 'I think it's time we both got some sleep.'

There was little point in further argument! Donna had to recognise that much. She left him standing there, too proud to let him see the frustrated tears gathering in her eyes. Why did this have to happen when everything had been going so well? Seeing Blake again was bad enough, but to do it in these circumstances went beyond all. He was punishing her, there was no doubt in her mind about that. Two years ago she had walked out on him, this time he was making sure she realised exactly who was in command of the initiative.

The tears had dried by the time she reached her room. They weren't going to get her anywhere. Only then did she realise she was still clutching the book she had taken from the case. She placed it on the bedside table, lowering herself to the edge of the mattress to sit gazing dully into space as shock began to catch up with her. Impossible to believe that the man she had left downstairs had ever held her in his arms; kissed her with warmth and with passion. He had given her so much, and yet so little. Six months, that was all it had taken. Start to finish in six short months. . .

The lecture had been well attended and gratifyingly received. Standing at her father's side during the aftermath of comment and congratulation, Donna found herself searching the sea of faces for that of the man she had first spotted during the slide show some half hour previously, finding him eventually over by the theatre doors. Barely thirty-two years of age, Blake Mitchell was already making a name for himself in the field of archaeology. Donna had seen a couple of magazine photographs, but this was the first time she had seen him in person. His dark, almost saturnine looks impressed her just as much as his professional reputation, she had to admit. Most professors of her acquaintance were of her father's age group.

He was lighting a cigarette right now, face bent to the flame of the lighter in his hand. The lift of his head brought his gaze into direct line with hers, one eyebrow quirking faintly as he registered her appraisal. Donna made herself hold that gaze for a lengthy moment before returning her own to the more immediate vicinity, aware of the swift hard thud of her heart. Attractive, yes, but there was more about him than that. Magnetism, it was called. She could feel it even from here.

He was still standing in the same place when her father made the move to break things up, taking her arm with a smiling apology to the people thronged about them.

'I'm sorry, but we really must be on our way,' he said in the deep cultured voice known to millions via his television appearances. 'I have another engagement this evening.'

'Do you plan on making another Peruvian expedition in the foreseeable future, Professor Campbell?' asked one man out of the crowd. 'You were saying you'd only scratched the surface so far.'

'I've no specific plans at the present,' admitted the older man smoothly. 'Finance is always a problem.' He was moving as he spoke, drawing Donna along with him. 'You'll excuse us for now.'

Farewells proffered were resigned to the inevitable, further questions stored against the next opportunity. Professor James Campbell was an important enough entity to set his own limitations. If he said that was all one had to accept it.

Seeing the tall, lean figure over by the doors straighten on their approach, Donna felt that same stirring of sensation in the pit of her stomach. She allowed herself a smile into steel-grey eyes as his glance flicked over her before steadying on her father's face.

'Congratulations,' he said. 'That was an excellent presentation.'

James Campbell accepted the compliment as his due, inclining his silver-flecked head graciously and just a trifle condescendingly towards the younger man. 'Glad you could make it after all. When did you get in?'

'Early this evening. I managed to get a flight at the last minute.' The explanation was no apology, just a simple statement of fact.

'You won't have had time for a meal, then?'

'Nothing substantial. Food can always wait.'

'More than I can, I'm afraid.' James hesitated, glancing at his watch. 'Do you have anywhere to stay?'

'Not yet. I came straight here from the airport.'

That elicited a smile. 'I'm glad to see you get your priorities right. Considering the time, you'd better let Donna take you back with her to the house. I've an appointment to keep.' He added briskly, 'We'll sort out details in the morning at the Museum, and fix you up with accommodation. Nice to have you with us.'

He was gone before Donna could say anything. Not that there was really anything much she could have said. Dumping problems into her lap was nothing new where her father was concerned. She had learned to cope. Only this was rather different. Thrown into a situation not of her own making, she found herself suddenly tongue-tied.

Her companion made the first move, drawing her out of the way of the departing audience with a hand lightly under an elbow. 'Your father forgot to introduce us,' he said. 'I'm Blake Mitchell.'

'I know.' She was recovering her composure. 'Professor Blake Mitchell, late of Harvard University. I hope you're going to enjoy working with my father— he isn't the easiest of taskmasters.'

His smile was brief. 'As one of the foremost authorities on Inca and Maya civilisations, I'd say he's entitled to demand a lot from his colleagues. The opportunity is the main thing.'

Having given up a lucrative teaching post in order to

grasp it, he had to be keen, Donna conceded. She knew quite a lot about Professor Mitchell—more than he probably realised. Like her father before him, he had gained both his B.A. and Ph.D. at Oxford, then gone on to postgraduate work in the States, including two years at the School of American Research in Santa Fe. He had been involved in three major expeditions in Peru and Bolivia and presented several notable papers before accepting the professorship at Harvard. In many ways it was a pity he had not been free to make this last field trip alongside her father, but there might be another time. Given the funding, the latter would return to Peru tomorrow. The land of the Incas was in his blood; it always had been.

'I think we'd better leave,' she said. 'They'll be closing the Institute any time now. I can give you a meal at home, if you can wait another half hour or so. It's only ten minutes by taxi.'

'Sounds good,' Blake agreed. 'My bags are with the porter.'

The hall porter procured a taxi for them within a few minutes. Seated in the rear of it, Donna said curiously, 'I gather you didn't come direct from the States.'

'No,' he conceded. 'I dropped off at Shannon to spend a couple of days with some old friends. There was some doubt whether I'd get here for the lecture— flights were fully booked. As it was, I only just made it.'

'But you did make it. Father will be pleased about that.'

'It was worth the effort.' He glanced her way in the semi-darkness, eyes lingering on the soft fullness of her mouth. 'You were with him for a time, weren't you?'

She nodded. 'Mostly as an onlooker, although I did a few drawings. I just got through art school.'

'No leanings towards archaeology?'

'Not enough staying power.' She made a small wry movement of her shoulders. 'I recognise my own limitations. What you and my father have been through to get where you are is beyond me.'

'There are non-graduate courses you could take.'

'I know. I'm considering draughtsmanship. Art is the only thing I'm any good at.'

'I wouldn't say that.' His tone was soft, the smile tensing nerve and sinew. 'You don't look a bit like your father.'

'I resemble my mother,' she responded, trying to keep a level head. 'She died some years ago.'

'She was an Egyptologist, wasn't she? That must have caused some clashing of interests at times.'

'You mean because of the differing areas?'

'I mean because she probably had little time for being a wife and mother. I've seen it happen before.'

Donna studied him for a long moment, registering the strength of character in the taut-skinned features. 'You think a wife should have no outside interests.'

'I think any woman should be prepared to make a choice between career and marriage—especially if she intends having children. I'd be willing to bet you spent a pretty deprived childhood yourself.'

He was too close to the mark for comfort, although nothing would have persuaded her to admit it. 'I didn't notice it,' she said. 'Did you live on campus at Harvard?'

The change of subject was accepted without objection, carrying them through the rest of the journey. Arriving at the terrace of Georgian houses a few moments later, Donna was first out of the vehicle, opening her purse with the intention of paying the driver.

'I'll see to that,' said Blake a trifle brusquely from behind her. He held out a couple of notes to the man at

the wheel before hauling the two leather suitcases from
the front compartment.

Donna closed her handbag again wryly. She had
grown so accustomed to handling all such minor
financial details in her father's company it hadn't
occurred to her to make allowances for male pride. If
she wanted to make anything of an impression on this
particular male she had better start considering it,
because he had a lot of it. And she did want to; there
was no getting away from that.

Indoors, she switched on a light in the deep hallway,
pleased with the welcoming effect of the white
woodwork and dark red carpeting. The nights were
turning cool now September was almost over.

'The guest room is second on the right on the first
floor,' she said. 'If you'd like to take your things up I'll
see about that meal.'

'Something light will do,' he responded. 'I ate on the
plane. Do I have time to change?'

'Of course. Say twenty minutes?' She was flicking
through the contents of the refrigerator in her mind as
she spoke. There were plenty of eggs and some left-over
chicken and ham. With the addition of a few prawns
and mushrooms she could make a Spanish omelette and
serve it with a tossed green salad. That should prove
substantial enough for the hour. If he wanted anything
else there was always the apple pie she had made
yesterday.

The way to a man's heart is through his stomach, she
thought whimsically, heading for the kitchen.

Blake had changed from the sober grey suit into jeans
and a blue sweat shirt when he came down again.
Donna served the meal in the kitchen dining alcove,
opening a bottle of wine on impulse to go with it. She
was hungry herself, she found, not having eaten since
four o'clock.

They talked about Peru while they ate, comparing notes on areas covered. The fever was in him too, Donna thought, watching his face as he spoke. Like her father, he came alive to the very mention of the ancient races. To return there in his company would really be something. She could only hope that the opportunity might one day arise. The research programme in which his aid had been enlisted was scheduled to take up the better part of a year, by which time she herself should have acquired some expertise. It was worth dreaming about.

They moved to the drawing room for coffee, pulling the curtains on the darkness outside and lighting a couple of lamps. Seated at Blake's side on the big, deep sofa, Donna was vitally aware of his closeness. Nothing in her life had prepared her for the impact this man had on her. She felt bemused and bewitched—incapable of rationalisation. If love at first sight could really happen, then she was in love. There was no other way to explain her emotions.

When he stopped talking suddenly and just sat there looking at her, she could only gaze right back, feeling her pulses start to race.

'You know,' he said softly, 'I've a feeling we're thinking the same thing right now. That mouth of yours is asking to be kissed.'

'Begging,' she corrected without shame or reticence. 'So why don't you put me out of my misery?'

She fitted into the curve of his arms easily, her own reaching up and around his neck to bring herself closer to the broad strong chest. His mouth was as she had imagined it, firm and searching, the pressure subtly increasing to part her lips. He ran the tip of his tongue along the edge of her teeth, sending ripple after ripple of sensation down her spine. Tentatively she touched him back, immediately withdrawing as his whole body tensed against her.

'Tantalising little devil,' he murmured against the corner of her mouth. 'You could be trouble.'

Donna said nothing as his hand pulled the hem of her blouse free of her skirt, wanting his touch with an urgency that blotted out all other considerations. She had been kissed enough times in her life for sure, but never known quite this degree of response. The feel of Blake's long, lean fingers on her skin made her shudder, though not with dread. She was glad of the firmness of her breast filling the palm of his hand, proud of her ability to bring a man like Blake Mitchell to the point of losing his professional cool. The whys and wherefores of what they were doing on so short an acquaintance were totally by the way. It felt right because the man was right. She had known that from the very first moment she had laid eyes on him. Not that she intended matters to go much further than this, regardless of how much she wanted them to. Blake was the kind of man a girl dreamed of having much much more than a casual affair with. The problem was going to be persuading him that she had something the other women he must have known in his thirty-two years had not.

Surprisingly it was Blake himself who called a halt, a hand still at her breast as he lifted his head to look down at her with searching eyes. 'Why me?' he asked. 'This quickly? I doubt if you're a girl who lets any Tom, Dick or Harry make love to her.'

'I'm not,' she assured him. 'I'm really not.' She put up a hand and touched the curve of his lower lip, senses stirring afresh as he took the tips of her two fingers into his mouth and softly imprisoned them for a moment. 'It's just that with you I can't help myself. I don't know why it should be like that. All I do know is how I felt when you looked at me across the lecture theatre tonight.'

'Tell me.'

She hesitated before putting it into words. 'As if,' she said at length, 'that something I'd been waiting for all my life had finally happened. Does that sound silly?'

'No.' His smile was slow. 'As a matter of fact, something similar happened to me too. I saw a lovely, nubile, golden-haired girl and I wanted her. Right there and then I wanted her. What does that make me?'

'A man who knows his own mind.' She returned the smile, feeling resolve harden inside her. Wanting was a long way from loving, but it was a very good start. She had to make Blake love her—she had to! She had never been as desperate about anything in her life. 'Blake, you're so different,' she whispered. 'I . . .'

'No,' he said again, 'no more analysis. There's going to be time for that later. For now let's settle for the fact that we both appear to share the same inclinations and indulge them some more . . .'

Indulge them they had, Donna thought, eyes still fixed unseeingly on the middle distance. But only up to a point. Morality had had little to do with her refusal to consummate her own growing desires over the following weeks. She had been playing for higher stakes. Only now could she appreciate that it would have made little difference in the long run. Blake had been as blind to their incompatibilities as she had.

Her father had been against the affair from the outset. It won't last, he had told her time and time again. You're confusing attraction with love. Later she had been able to see the truth in that statement; right then she hadn't wanted to know. Marrying Blake had become a major obsession.

The honeymoon had been short but idyllic, the return to earth somewhat less so. Unlike her father, Blake had been prepared to share no more than the bare periphery of his work with her, and keeping the flat he had leased spick and span scarcely taxed her resources to the limit. When, bored and restless, she had proposed a return to her studies, however, the suggestion had been met with blank rejection on Blake's part. She could remember the scene as if it were only yesterday, every word indelibly imprinted . . .

'You made your choice when you married me,' he said bluntly. 'I want a wife, not a college student.'

'And I want to be involved, not just a bystander on any coming dig!' Donna protested. 'I could even illustrate the book you're planning to write one of these days.'

'The last thing I need on any dig is that kind of emotional distraction.' His tone was flat. 'I don't believe a husband and wife should live in each other's pockets, or even necessarily share the same interests. Anyway, I thought we'd agreed that starting a family early was a good idea.'

'We did, and I still want to. Only twenty-three or even four should be plenty early enough.'

'Not for me—I'm thirty-two already. The time is now, if any.' He looked at her lying in the wide double bed which almost filled the bedroom of the flat, his slow smile appreciative of the sight. 'In fact, right now seems a very good idea!'

Donna smiled too as he came towards her, a hint of malice in her eyes. 'You forget, I'm on the pill.'

'Then we'll have to see about getting you off it.' He came down on top of her, putting his lips to her eyes, to her temple, feathering them oh, so softly down the curve of her cheek and along her jawbone to find her mouth in a kiss she could no more hold out against than fly. The hands seeking her breasts were possessive, fully aware of their power to rouse.

'I mean it,' he murmured a little later against her lips. 'I want children, Donna. A marriage needs children.'

At that precise moment Donna was beyond arguing the point. Blake's lovemaking left little to be desired.

Confirmation of her pregnancy some weeks later brought mixed feelings. While part of her wanted this baby, another part already rejected it. It was Blake's way of tying her down. With a child to take care of there was no chance of furthering her career.

Her father heard the news with anger and disappointment. 'You could have waited,' he stormed. 'You're only just twenty-one years old! What about all the plans we made—the things we were going to do together?'

'The difference being that you're you and Blake has other ideas,' she responded heavily. 'He wants a proper home with resident wife and two planned children.'

'Didn't he tell you all this before you married him?'

'No . . . Well, not in quite the same way.' She spread her hands helplessly. 'I knew he wanted children, I didn't think it would be quite so soon, that's all.'

'Then you should have refused to make it possible. Good heavens, child, I surely don't have to tell you how!'

'That was no answer. It simply caused trouble between us.'

James Campbell shook his head in disgust. 'So you simply let him have things his own way. Are you so besotted by him that you've lost all your initiative?'

'I don't know,' she confessed. 'I honestly don't know what I feel for him right now. That's why I came to see you first.'

Her father's eyes took on a sudden new expression. 'You mean he doesn't know yet?'

'Not for sure. He probably suspects. He's well

enough acquainted with female physiology to have noted dates.'

'Then don't have it.' James spoke rapidly as if to get the words out before she could interrupt. 'I can arrange . . .'

'No!' Donna was on her feet, hands pressed unconsciously against her stomach as if in protection of her unborn child. 'I'd never do that! Not for *any* reason.'

It was her father's turn to spread his hands. 'Then what?'

'I have to have it, of course.' She attempted a smile. 'Perhaps it will bring us closer again.'

'And perhaps it might not.' He searched her face, his own strained. 'Donna, why don't you leave him and come on back home? At least your life would be your own again.'

'With a baby?'

'We'd get someone in to look after it if you decided to go on with your career after all.'

'And what about your work together, you and Blake? Where would that come in?'

'It wouldn't.' He shrugged wryly. 'I'm not going to pretend I've gained nothing from our partnership this past few months. He's a clever and knowledgeable man. But you're my main concern. I want my daughter back, Donna. We had such plans!'

Donna elected to walk part of the way back to the flat, needing time to think. Less than six months of marriage and already it was on the verge of failure. This baby was no real answer; the rift went too deep. Her father had been right all along. It was fascination rather than love that had been the drawing force so far as she was concerned. Blake could still move her physically, it was true, but there was nothing else. He didn't need her the way her father needed her. All he had ever wanted . . .

Donna winced even now at the remembered screech of brakes, the sudden tearing pain as the car wing had caught her a glancing blow. The accident had been entirely her own fault. There had been witnesses to the way she had stepped straight off the pavement without looking. She had been lucky, considering. Apart from a badly bruised hip and leg she had escaped serious injury. But she had lost the baby . . .

She was standing at the window when Blake came to fetch her home on the fifth day.

'I'm not coming,' she said without turning. 'It's over, Blake. We both know it.'

'You're talking nonsense,' he returned evenly, staying where he was. 'You've had a bad time, but you'll get over it. There was no permanent damage.'

'You mean I can always have other babies?' This time she did bring her head round, eyes devoid of emotion. 'Is that all it meant to you?'

'I never had the opportunity to think about it in any personal sense,' he said on the same level note. 'Your father had that privilege. In future I'd be grateful if you'd tell me what you're thinking and feeling first.'

'The way you share with me?' She shook her head. 'There isn't going to be any future, I'm going home. My *own* home.'

'If that's what you want.' His face was hard. 'I'm going back to the States. If you change your mind you're welcome to come with me.'

Donna stared at him. 'When was that decided?'

'Let's say your father decided for me.' He was opening the door as he spoke. 'I shan't press you, Donna. You have to know what you want. I'll be leaving on Sunday. All you have to do is phone me.'

Someone was knocking softly on the bedroom door. Donna dragged herself slowly back from the past, eyes seeking the dial of the clock on the bedside table. Almost three, she registered in disbelief. She had been sitting here thinking for nearly an hour.

The tapping came again, still soft but somehow more insistent. The only other person up and around that she knew of was Blake, and he was the last one she wanted to see, yet it was obvious that the caller was not going to go away. What he could want she couldn't begin to think. They had said all there was to say downstairs.

He was still dressed in the cord jacket and slacks when she opened the door. The only difference lay in the faint relaxation of hardness about his mouth and jawline.

'I took a chance on finding you,' he said. 'This was the only door with a light under it.'

'You're next door,' she returned, keeping her voice as low as his. She indicated. 'That way.'

'Okay, that's fine. Only first I wanted to talk to you.'

Donna looked at him for a long moment without blinking. 'I thought you already did that.'

'I was in shock—we both were. I've had time to think things over since.' Blake moved forward before she could attempt to close the door in his face, taking it from her as she stepped involuntarily backward and confining them both in the room. 'What I said earlier about not taking you with us tomorrow, let's forget it. You were right—personal feelings don't have any bearing.'

If anything the shock was greater this time. Donna barely knew how to react. 'Why?' she got out at length. 'Why change your mind now?'

'I told you.' The grey eyes gave little away. 'I had time to consider. I'd have left it till morning if I hadn't seen your light. Leaving you to stew all night seemed unfair.'

Something was breaking up slowly deep inside her, a cautious warmth beginning to steal through her veins. 'I'm grateful,' she said, and meant it. 'You won't regret it.'

Blake's smile was faint. 'I don't intend to. If John Brinkman was satisfied with your capabilities then that's good enough for me. We leave for Cuzco after lunch.'

'Yes, I know.' Donna hesitated as he began to turn back to the door, moved by some emotion she didn't attempt to define. 'Blake, I'm sorry it had to be this way.'

'Yes,' he agreed without looking at her, 'so am I. We'll just have to make the best of it.'

CHAPTER TWO

DESPITE the events of the night, Donna was up and dressed by seven. Too restless to stay in her room until summoned to breakfast, she made her way downstairs, emerging from the rear of the house into a morning of grey mist and humid heat.

The grounds proved to be extensive, stretching to the cliffs overlooking the Pacific. She strolled back slowly, trying to come to grips with conflicting emotions. She wanted to continue with this job, of course, but Blake's presence was not to be lightly put aside. Graham knew the details of her marriage if no one else did. There would be no keeping the relationship secret from him once he heard the name Mitchell. She had to tell him first, before he heard the news through others.

She had the opportunity because he was standing on the veranda when she reached the house. He came down to meet her, drawing her close to kiss her with the quiet warmth that was so much a part of his nature.

'You're an early bird,' he said. 'Why didn't you wake me?'

'I needed to be alone,' Donna admitted. She laid her face against his shoulder for a moment, drawing strength from him before pushing herself resignedly upright again. 'Graham, there's been a change in the team. Blake is here.'

'Your husband?' He sounded blank and uncomprehending. 'Why? I thought the team was complete.'

'He's taking over as director. Dr Brinkman broke an ankle.' She kept her tone matter-of-fact. 'I was looking

for a book downstairs when he arrived last night—or I
should say early this morning. It was ... quite a
surprise.'

'It must have been.' Graham was looking at her now
with sympathy and concern. 'You're trying to tell me he
wants you out of the team, is that it?'

'He did.' She paused. 'Then he changed his mind.'

'Oh?' He was nonplussed. 'Well, that's something.
From what you've told me about him he isn't the type
to do that very often.' He was silent, appearing to be
summing up the situation. When he did speak it was on
a different note. 'It's a hell of a time for it to happen,
but it might not be such a bad thing in the long run.
You could take the opportunity to tell him you want a
divorce.'

'It's hardly the right time for that,' she protested.
'Last night we agreed that personal relationships had to
be kept out of it.'

'Hardly possible in the circumstances. I'd say the sooner
things were settled between the two of you the better.'

'After two years a few more weeks aren't going to
make a lot of difference.'

'They are to me.' He brought up a hand to smooth
back the fall of hair from her face, eyes questioning. 'I
want to marry you, Donna. Now's good a time as any
to say it. You know how I feel about you, I think you
feel the same way about me. Am I wrong?'

She was shaken, not adequately prepared for a
declaration of this kind. She said slowly, 'I do think a
lot of you, Graham. You've been my mainstay since my
father died. I just didn't ...' she paused, searching for
the right words, finding only lame ones '... didn't
realise you had marriage in mind.'

'You mean you wouldn't let yourself think about it.
Not with the problems to be faced.' He shook his head,
gentle but determined. 'You can't spend the rest of your

life afraid to try again. You and Blake failed because you were incompatible. We have so much in common. We'd be a team in every sense of the word—working together, travelling together.'

'What about children?' she asked, trying to sort out the confusion in both heart and mind. 'Wouldn't you want a family?'

'Of course, but there's plenty of time. And kids don't need to be a complete tie if things are organised right.'

It had been Blake's assumption that her rightful place was in the home looking after his children that had contributed to the break-up of their marriage in the first place, so why should she feel now that Graham's attitude left something to be desired? He accepted her as his equal in every sphere.

'Can't we just leave things the way they are for now?' she asked. 'We can hardly start divorce proceedings from eight thousand feet up!' She put a hand on his arm, looking up pleadingly into his face. 'Just see this job through first.'

His agreement came with reluctance. Donna was relieved to hear the gong summoning them in to breakfast. Graham had presented her with yet another problem.

Most of the party had already assembled in the dining room by the time they reached it, but there was no sign of Blake. Donna was on the verge of announcing the news when he walked in. He was dressed in jeans and a cotton shirt which moulded his muscular frame, but there was nothing casual in his manner.

His explanation caused comment among the assembly but little consternation. The aim remained the same no matter who headed the team. Janine Meade appeared to be the only one who actually knew him on a personal basis. Watching the two of them exchange greetings, Donna was aware of a sudden tautness in her chest.

More than a simple working relationship, if she was any judge. There was something almost proprietorial in the way the woman swept him along to a seat at her side.

Only as she met the grey eyes herself did it register that this was not the same man who had come to her room last night. His expression was hard as iron. Something had happened between then and now to cause that change, it was obvious, yet what? She was at a loss to explain it.

From the snatches of conversation audible across the table, she was able to gather that he and Janine Meade had been together on an expedition to Bolivia the year before, following the trail of the Incas who had fled from the Spanish invasion.

'There's no conclusive evidence that the Inca civilisation lived on in anything but isolated pockets,' said Blake in answer to a query from one of the other younger men who was also listening in. 'We found no cities of gold.' The last with an ironic little smile. 'Only the romantics still believe in El Dorado!'

And only fools let romance govern any portion of their lives, thought Donna with cynicism.

The party gathered in the salon after breakfast for an orientation talk during which various aspects of the work to be undertaken were discussed.

'We don't have any aerial views of the site,' Blake told Graham at one point. 'While we're stuck in Cuzco you could take the opportunity to fly over and see what you can do. I'll organise a charter.'

'An artist's impression could be valuable too,' said Graham.

'Perhaps.' The tone was short. 'If there are no questions we may as well leave things there. Lunch will be at twelve sharp. We leave for the airport at one-thirty.'

Most of the party dispersed to their respective rooms at that point for last-minute sorting of gear and equipment. Donna escaped from Graham on the same pretext, sitting for some length of time gathering nerve. There had to be a reason for Blake's change of attitude this morning, and she had to know what it was. Surely he couldn't already be regretting the gesture he had made last night?

All was quiet when she eventually made the short journey to the next room up the corridor, hoping Blake was still inside. Her knock was answered almost immediately, her visit seemingly half anticipated if his total lack of surprise on seeing her standing there was anything to go by.

'For someone as anxious as you are to keep our relationship a secret, you're taking a chance,' he said coolly. 'You'd better come in before you're seen.'

'It isn't a case of secretiveness so much as avoiding unnecessary explanations,' Donna responded, accepting the invitation. 'There's no reason for anyone to know about us.'

'Including your lover?' He spoke quietly enough, but the edge was there. 'Does Horsley even know you're married?'

'He knows.' She had lost colour momentarily; now it flooded back. 'Graham knows everything. And he isn't my lover.'

'That wasn't the impression I gained from what I saw from my window earlier. There was an air of long familiarity in the way he kissed you. You're not going to deny you were acquainted well before this trip got under way?'

'Of course I'm not going to deny it,' she said. 'Why should I?'

'Because the question of motivation might come under some suspicion.' The pause was too brief for interruption. 'Did he have anything to do with your getting the job in the first place?'

Donna hesitated, too well aware where all this was leading. 'That isn't really relevant. Dr Brinkman . . .'

'*Did* he?' Blake cut in like a whiplash. 'Just give me a straight answer.'

She drew in a steadying breath, determined to face him out. 'Graham sent samples of my work and suggested I might be a suitable candidate, yes. If I hadn't come up to par no word of his would have made any difference.'

'It isn't the quality of work I'm disputing,' he said. 'What I object to is the inclusion of any man's mistress on a scientific expedition.'

'Damn you, Blake!' Her eyes blazed. 'If I *were* his mistress you still wouldn't have the right to say what you are saying! Graham recommended me for the job because he had confidence in my abilities as an artist, not because he wanted someone to keep him warm at nights! Any relationship between us is purely incidental.'

'It looked anything but this morning.'

'He asked me to marry him,' she said, goaded beyond endurance. 'It's an emotional moment—or had you forgotten?'

'I hadn't forgotten.' Blake was in control, and dangerous with it. 'What did you tell him?'

'I said I'd think about it later, after we get back.'

'One small factor you *both* seem to have forgotten. You already have one husband. Or is that incidental too?'

'No.' She looked him squarely in the eye. 'You asked me last night why I'd never done anything about a divorce. Well, I'm doing it now. I want one, Blake, as soon as it can be arranged. I realise we're stuck with the situation for the time being, but at least we can set the wheels in motion as soon as we get back to England.'

'Always providing I agree.' He had his hands in his

pockets as he spoke, mouth set in a thin hard line. 'You take too much for granted, Donna. You always did.'

She gazed at him in silence for what seemed an age, unable to comprehend the depths of the anger in him. 'We've been separated for two years,' she got out at last. 'Whether you like it or not, that gives me adequate grounds.'

'Only where the application is uncontested. The desertion, I might remind you, was yours, not mine. Oh, you'd get it eventually, I've no doubt, but it's going to take time and money. Can you afford it?'

Had she ever really known this man? Donna wondered numbly, studying the iron jawline, the cruelly narrowed eyes. He was doing this deliberately; wanting to hurt her.

'Why?' she demanded. 'What profit can you gain from making things difficult?'

'The satisfaction of putting you through a little of what I went through two years ago—if in a slightly different manner.' The words were soft and deadly. 'Have you any idea what it was like to lose a wife and child at one and the same time? I spent three days in that flat of ours waiting for a phone call that never came.'

'You were going back to the States,' she whispered.

'Only because you'd made it plain to your father that he could have you back if he got rid of me.'

'That isn't true!'

'No?' He studied her cynically, taking in the vulnerability of her mouth. 'You didn't tell him you'd never leave England on any permanent basis?'

'I may have said that some time.' She made a small gesture of appeal. 'You have it all wrong anyway. I'd decided to leave you before I knew you were going.'

'But there was a chance we might have got together again if your father hadn't given me my marching orders.'

'It wasn't his doing. You were employed by the Museum.'

'In his department and on his request. Don't take me for an idiot, Donna. I may have been all sorts of a fool where you were concerned, but you cured me of that— you and your father between you.'

'Blake, don't!' Donna was trembling all over now, limbs as heavy as her heart. 'I was so terribly confused. I didn't know how I felt about anything. You . . . we married too soon. We should have waited.'

'For what? You to grow up? Yes, maybe you're right. Only you didn't make it easy to wait, did you? For your age, you were one of the finest bait-hookers I'd ever come across!'

'So you married me because you couldn't have me any other way.' Contempt was a saving grace, affording her the luxury of self-righteousness. 'You were twelve years older. Mature enough, or should have been, to see I was only infatuated with you. But no, not you. You saw what *you* wanted—a young, unused body you could teach all your foul tricks to! Professor Mitchell, the great sexologist! I wonder how many of your female students benefited from the extra tuition!'

There was a blur of movement and two hands clamped hard about her upper arms, jerking her towards him. His mouth was savage, forcing hers open. Then he was pushing her backwards and she felt the edge of the bed behind her knees, the loss of balance which sent her crashing down on her back with his weight on top of her.

The material of her shirt ripped all too easily, baring her breasts to his cruel fingers. She twisted desperately beneath him as he rammed a knee between her thighs, feeling his strength, aware of his arousal. This couldn't be happening—not to her! She wanted to cry out for help, yet no sound would come.

As abruptly as he had seized her, Blake let her go, shoving himself roughly to his feet and putting distance between them.

'You'd better get out of here,' he growled, 'while you still can!'

Clutching the torn shirt about her, Donna rose to a sitting position. Her lips felt swollen and bruised, her whole body violated. That was the closest she had ever come to rape, and the closest she ever wanted to be.

'If there was little love lost between us before there has to be even less now,' she whispered with loathing. 'Just *who* do you think you are, Blake?'

'A man who just came very close to losing his grip,' he admitted. 'The fact that you asked for it is totally by the way.' He didn't move from where he stood, body rigidly under control. 'Are you going to go, or do I have to throw you out?'

'Am I supposed to just forget about this?'

'No.' His glance was calculated to freeze. 'I want you to remember, and remember well. Push me too far and next time I might not be capable of stopping!'

'There won't be a next time.' She was on her feet now, though still weak at the knees. 'Graham will see to that!'

'Graham will see to nothing—particularly not you. If I catch any hint of contact between you outside of the job itself I'll have him on a plane home before he can blink!'

Donna's chin lifted sharply. 'I doubt if you have that much authority.'

'Try me,' he invited. 'If you want that divorce you're going to have to suffer a little frustration for it. So is your boy-friend. He's a good photographer, but there are others.'

'You know, it's odd,' she said, 'of all the things I might once have called you, vindictive wasn't among them. It just goes to show how misguided one can be!'

Blake made no attempt to reply to that parting shot. Fortunately the corridor was still empty. Safely inside her own room, Donna took off the cotton shirt and stuffed it into a corner of her suitcase. They would be leaving all extra items of luggage behind in Cuzco when they set off on the final stage of the journey. Even if the buttonholes had not been ripped beyond repair she would never want to wear it again.

Her fingers still trembled as she fastened herself into another plain cotton shirt and exchanged her linen skirt for serviceable cord jeans in a dark beige. In trousers she felt safer, less vulnerable to attack. Not that she intended giving Blake any further excuse to humiliate her. The memory of his hands touching her so intimately was almost more than she could bear.

Only in the dimmest recesses of her mind dared she admit to the truth. Devoid of all tenderness though his caresses had been, they had awakened in her sensations too long repressed. There had even been a moment when she had wanted him to go on; to finish what he had started. Purely chemical, of course, but dangerous just the same. Fulfilment of that nature would be all too shortlived.

Blake looked totally in control of himself at lunch. Watching him surreptitiously, Donna could scarcely believe that the events of a couple of hours ago had actually happened. The tenderness of her lips and breasts, however, was indisputable evidence to the contrary. She would have bruises tomorrow for sure; the marks where his fingers had gripped her arms were already in the process of turning blue. In long sleeves they remained hidden, but she would have some explaining to do if Graham caught sight of them. Certainly he would never be capable of inflicting bruises. His gentleness with her was one of the things she loved about him. Yes, *loved*. It was time she put a name to the emotion he aroused in her.

They travelled out to the airport in several taxis. Blake was in with Janine Meade and Edith Remington. Surprisingly he had made no attempt to part Donna from Graham.

By three o'clock they were in the air, clearing the last remnants of coastal fog as they headed for the rugged mountain slopes. Everywhere looked parched and brown, although there was the occasional glimmer of water deep in a canyon. Further on where the ground became wetter and more fertile, tiny plots of cultivated land clung to the hillsides, then they were climbing again to clear the bulk of the Andes, and range after breathtaking range lay as far as eye could see to every side.

'Awe-inspiring, isn't it?' commented Edith Remington from across the aisle. 'I gather you've seen it before?'

'Three years ago,' Donna agreed. 'I was with my father then.' She smiled at Graham seated by her side in order to reassure him that this time with him was no less of an experience. 'We should be there in about twenty minutes.'

They approached their destination from the north across the famous Inca battlefield of Anta, seeing the ground fall away beneath them to reveal the red-tiled city, studded with domes and spires. Guarded by the massive boulders of the fortress and the giant white-painted statue of Christ standing with arms out-stretched, it made an impressive sight.

At eleven thousand feet above sea-level, the air was thin and sharp, creating instant breathlessness. There were tourists of many nationalities in the streets, along with the Cuzqueños in their dark suits and fedora hats and Quechua Indians wearing hand-woven ponchos. A group of students made their way noisily along the Avenue of the Sun, heading for the Plaza de Armas which was the central square of the city. Four years were as nothing in this part of the world, acknowledged Donna, seeking familiar landmarks. It could have been yesterday she was here.

This time they were to be billeted in a house owned by the Institute of Archaeology just off the Plaza Cabildo. Built of the same pinkish volcanic stone the Incas had used, it boasted a superb Baroque doorway. Donna knew many of these older buildings had been damaged in the 1950 earthquake, but this one had been beautifully restored.

Inside was spartan compared with the Lima house, but with enough mod cons to make life perfectly comfortable. Accommodation was by pairs owing to the limitation of available rooms. With three women on the team, the division was obvious. Donna would have preferred to share with Edith Remington, but it was taken for granted that the older woman merited the privacy. Janine seemed no more thrilled with the arrangement, tossing her bag on to the nearest of the two narrow beds with an air of resignation.

'Three days of this place will be more than enough,' she exclaimed. 'Those of us who've been at this height before hardly need that much acclimatisation!'

'But those who haven't do,' said Donna, taking the other bed. '*Soroche* is no joke. Anyway, there's all the equipment to sort.'

'That won't take three days either.'

Donna was silent, not prepared to argue the point. Three days was a long time, true, but she had a feeling that John Brinkman had intended to give his team the breathing space for a purpose. Although the site was less than a hundred miles away as the crow flies, transportation difficulties were going to make it impossible to visit the city on any unessential business. They would be living in tents for weeks to come, with recreational activities limited to the available company and surroundings. A little pre-relaxation would not go amiss.

Janine stripped off the clothes in which she had travelled, revealing a well-exercised figure. 'I'm going to have a shower,' she announced, reaching for a towel and wrap. 'We're supposedly eating early to give us all maximum rest this first night.' She paused at the door, glancing back to where Donna stood by her bed wrestling with the straps of her suitcase. 'Just for the record, are you and our photographer together?'

'We came together,' Donna returned, not bothering to look round. 'Any other questions?'

'Just a reminder that you're a very minor member of this team, easily replaced. I saw you go to Professor Mitchell's room this morning. What was the idea?'

'My own business.' Donna still made no attempt to turn her head. 'If you're so curious, and think you have a right to know, why not ask Professor Mitchell himself?'

'I might do just that. The last thing he needs is an amateur on his back.'

'I'm sure it's the very last thing he'd allow himself,' Donna said smoothly. 'I shouldn't worry too much about our Director's welfare if I were you. He seems well able to take care of himself.'

Round one to her, she thought as the door closed sharply after the other woman. Janine had an inflated sense of her own importance on this mission. No, that wasn't really true, she had to concede immediately. Janine was important to the mission—very important. Her knowledge and experience gave her a very high billing in the order of things. All the same, art work had its own place, and a very necessary one. Providing she did her job well enough no one had any right to try putting her down.

There was more to it than that, though, wasn't there?

Her visit to Blake had been the real reason behind that little outburst. Janine had been warning her off, not just professionally but personally too. She had her eye on Blake for herself. There was nothing more obvious than that. What a shock it would be if the truth were ever revealed.

Dinner was at seven-thirty, served in a long white-walled room furnished in heavily carved dark wood and hung with religious paintings scattered liberally with gold dust.

'Barnardo Bitti,' murmured Graham, nodding to one of the nearest canvases depicting the Virgin suckling an infant Jesus wearing an Indian cap. 'Could be a copy, I suppose. The original must be worth a hefty sum.'

'I didn't realise you were knowledgeable in Peruvian art,' said Donna, surprised.

He grinned. 'I'm not. I just happened to see an illustration in a book through there in the salon. Some of us are willing to spend time improving the mind as well as the looks. Not that the result of your efforts isn't appreciated. We'll be seeing the last of female legs for a few weeks this next couple of days.'

'Uncovered ones, anyway,' she agreed. 'Tomorrow I'm going to show you round Cuzco. It's one time I have an edge on you.'

'You always have an edge on me,' he responded softly, and briefly covered her hand where it lay on the cloth between them. 'Don't expect me to wait out the whole dig without at least kissing you, will you? That would be more than flesh and blood could stand!'

Donna's eyes were drawn by force to the top of the table where Blake sat, meeting his gaze without flinching. So let him see. Why should she care? His threats held little weight out here. With deliberation she looked back to Graham's face and smiled a slow, warm smile. 'More than mine could stand too, I think.'

If any of the party had entertained ideas of going out to view the city at closer quarters by night they were all too quickly dispelled by the general fatigue experienced by all before the evening was halfway through. Donna had a headache, and knew she was probably not alone. She was glad to finish the meal with the *mate de coca*, a drink looking like tea but made from coca leaves which the locals would chew to counteract the effects of high altitude.

With no previous acclimatisation to aid him, Graham was even worse affected, admitting to dizziness when they parted at Donna's bedroom door.

'You'll feel better by morning,' she assured him, sympathising. 'We all will. It's just a matter of getting used to breathing at a different pace and depth.' She reached up and kissed him lightly on the lips. 'Goodnight, Graham.'

'Try darling,' he requested with a wry smile. 'I'm in need of some comfort to take to my bed tonight!'

Donna had been in bed more than an hour before Janine came to the room. Eyes closed, she heard the other girl say goodnight softly to someone out in the corridor, and was pretty sure the companion was Blake. Where they had been and what they had been doing she told herself she didn't care, and knew she lied. Physically, Blake still had the power to stir her, to make her remember what it had been like with him. The thought of him so much as touching Janine gave rise to feelings she could only liken to jealousy—or would dog-in-the-manger be closer the mark? Perhaps he too should remember he was married still.

CHAPTER THREE

UNLIKE Lima's climate, the day was bright and warm, similar to an English summer's day at its very best. The whole group was up at an early hour, most professing to feeling better.

Donna set off alone with Graham to make the short walk to the Plaza de Armas, finding the square already crowded. Wooden stalls piled high with produce were doing a brisk trade, the bargaining loud and clamorous. A couple of Indians sat in serious conversation on the steps of the seventeenth-century cathedral, wearing the breeches, ponchos and traditional felt hats of the outlying villages. Graham photographed everything and everyone, clicking away like the true professional. He might, Donna knew, eventually finish up with just a couple of shots he considered worthwhile, but the saturation technique at least assured that little opportunity was lost.

The narrow street they took from the square was bounded on both sides by the original Inca walling, huge blocks of dull brown rock fitted together without cement and practically impervious to earthquake shock. At one intersection they came across a brick-built cinema with a programme already in progress, judging from the sounds issuing forth. Hollywood was everywhere, as Graham dryly remarked.

It was somewhere around the site of the Temple of the Sun that they lost touch with each other. Donna had moved away from him for a moment or two to look into the rooms where the mummies of dead Emperors had once been deposited, and when she turned back he was gone, swallowed up by the milling throngs of people. Looking for him was hopeless, although she did try for a while. There was little point in worrying about it, she decided eventually. Graham was perfectly capable of finding his own way back to the house. In the meantime it was approaching noon and she was hungry again. One thing Cuzco did not lack was restaurants.

She was on the point of leaving the monastery which now occupied the site when Blake appeared from nowhere. He was unaccompanied, his jeans and tee-shirt as casual as her own. There was no element of surprise in his eyes when he saw her.

'Have you been following me?' she demanded coolly as he joined her. 'You won't have found the exercise very productive.'

'I've been to see an old friend who's working on the excavations here,' he returned. 'Coincidences do happen.' He cast a glance around, brows lifting. 'All alone?'

'In this crowd?' Her tone was short. 'Hardly.'

'I'm talking about the boy-friend, as you very well know. You left the house together.'

'Observant of you.' She began to move away, only to be brought up short by the fingers fastening on her arm. Quivering with something deeper than anger, she snatched herself free. 'Don't touch me, Blake! You did enough of that yesterday!'

'And I'm not apologising for it,' he returned hardily. 'You'd had it coming for a long time. Have you eaten yet?'

'No,' she snapped. 'And I'm not doing it with you.'

'You'll do anything I tell you to do. Either that or you go right on home.' His eyes were hard as agates. 'In case you'd forgotten, I hold the reins out here. You're not irreplaceable.'

Her laugh had a cracked sound. 'Oh, I'm sure that's true—in any sphere! Can you remember how many women you've had since I walked out?' She gave him no time to reply, ignoring the danger signal in the tensing of his jawline. 'Dr Meade, for instance? Don't tell me that's a purely professional relationship!'

Blake made no answer to that, grasping her by the arm again to pull her rapidly along with him as he strode from the building. Conscious of the attention they were attracting, Donna stopped fighting and let herself be drawn, secure in the knowledge that little could happen to her on the streets. Provoking Blake this way was dangerous and it was cheap, but she couldn't seem to stop herself.

She had reckoned without his knowledge of the city. The narrow *calle* into which he dragged her was deserted. Pinned against the rough stone by the weight of his body, she twisted her face away from his, but he simply took her jaw in his hand to hold her still to his punishing kiss.

'I don't have to take that kind of innuendo from you,' he gritted. 'Not without doing something about it!'

'What about the things you accused me of with Graham?' she got out through freshly bruised lips. 'Is there any difference?'

'There is to me. And I don't give a damn what's fair and what isn't!' He was still holding her against the wall, the hardness of his body trapping her breath. The taut muscularity of his thighs brought back memories Donna preferred to forget. Or did she? There was a heat at the pit of her stomach, a spreading fire no willpower could control. She wanted to move against him; to rouse him the same way he was rousing her. It wouldn't take much. Anger itself was an aphrodisiac of sorts.

'Blake, let me go,' she whispered. 'This isn't doing either of us any good.'

Surprisingly he obeyed, moving away from her with a faint curl of his lip. 'You don't change,' he said. 'Be thankful I have. Now, come and eat.'

She accompanied him without further argument, trying to work out what he might have meant by that last remark. In what way had he changed? Was he referring to his lack of feeling for her? Certainly there had been a time when just to be that close would have elicited at least a physical response. Yesterday was something else again; she hardly wanted a repeat performance. Yet the ache inside her was not to be ignored. Was there something wrong with her that she could respond to violence from a man she hated? Graham could rouse her, true, but never to quite the same degree. Suddenly she wished herself anywhere but this place.

They ate at a small restaurant whose menu was written on a blackboard at the door. Donna chose crisp pork with tiny spiced potatoes, refusing the maize jelly offered for dessert and settling instead for another cup of the *mate de coca*. They had spoken little during the meal. Now, with the cups on the table before them, Blake leaned back in his chair and gave her an enigmatic look.

'Got your breath back yet?'

Donna toyed with the handle of her cup, aware that he was deliberately baiting her. No doubt he had recognised her reaction in the alley—recognised, and was amused by it. She lifted her eyes to meet his with purpose, refusing to acknowledge the mockery.

'I've been here before, remember. It gives a certain immunity. When do we actually leave for Incanta?'

'Thursday, with luck. Tomorrow I plan on taking the whole team to Machu Picchu for a preview. Apparently the layout is similar to Incanta, though on a rather larger scale.'

'Competing with the tourists?'

'Ignoring them where possible.' He drank his coffee, watching her raise her own cup to her lips. 'You realise that stuff forms the basis for cocaine?'

'But in this form it isn't a drug, just a mild, natural stimulant,' she responded smartly. 'Gone are the days when I needed a mentor. I'm more than capable of taking care of my own good health!'

'You're capable of a whole lot of things,' he agreed. 'But I'm not sure common sense is among them. Don't keep challenging me, Donna, I'm likely to take you up on it.'

She studied him warily, seeing the way the light fell across the strongly chiselled features. A face to fit its surrounding, she thought. There was almost the look of the Inca about him. For a fleeting moment the past was close, the very air vibrant with sounds and scents alien to her senses. Blake was right, she conceded, pulling herself together; she was drinking too much *coca*.

'Why can't we simply let bygones be bygones?' she asked, striving for a reasonable note. 'Whoever was at fault initially, we're not going to change anything by being enemies now. You have your life to live and I have mine.'

'As simple as that?' He shook his head, expression unrelenting. 'You still owe me, Donna, and you're going to pay—one way or another.'

She said with care, 'I'm not sure what that means exactly. How many ways are there?'

'Enough. Putting a stop to your divorce plans is only one of them.' He paused a moment, eyes on her face with something unfathomable in their depths. 'You see, I still want you. Physically, at least.'

'That was evident a short while ago.' The words were out before she could think about it, drawing a faint sardonic smile.

'You noticed? But then the venue was hardly conducive. If I'm nothing else I'm practical. We're going to be seeing a lot of each other these coming weeks, and the nights can be pretty cold up here.'

He was playing games with her, Donna concluded. This was the man talking, not the archaeologist.

'Hardly what you said the other night,' she reminded him. 'The situation doesn't lend itself to working conditions. Wasn't that it?'

'That was then, when I was still in shock, this is now when I'm not. The job won't suffer.'

She didn't believe a word of it. Once on site his thirst for knowledge would overrule everything else. A part of her regretted that assurance, she had to admit. When it came to making love there would never be anyone to match Blake. Graham was a wonderful and considerate person, but he didn't excite her. Yet wouldn't that relationship prove a better basis for a lasting and happy marriage in the end? Excitement faded, contentment grew.

'I think it's time we were getting back,' she said. 'People are going to be wondering where we are.'

'Meaning Horsley.' His shrug was indifferent. 'He knows the facts. He can hardly complain.'

'What about Janine?' she asked blandly. 'Does she have grounds for complaint?'

'If she did she'd have the sense to keep them to herself.' He tossed a handful of notes on to the table and stood up. 'So let's get back.'

It was a longish walk back to the house, and not a chatty one. Graham came out from the salon as they went indoors, face expressing his emotions all too clearly when he saw who Donna was with.

'I've been back ages,' he said. 'Where did you get to all this time?'

'I took my wife for lunch,' Blake put in before Donna could answer. 'Hardly an unusual occurrence.

Incidentally, I've set up that air reconnaissance for tomorrow—two o'clock at the airport. Ask for a Señor Coba, he'll be flying you over the site.'

'I thought we were all going to Machu Picchu tomorrow,' said Donna.

'The rest of us are. There are enough photographs of that place to fill several books already.'

'Janine Meade was here a while back looking for you,' said Graham as the other man started towards the staircase. 'She seemed to think you had some arrangement.'

'Thanks.' Blake didn't even pause in his stride.

Donna moved forward past Graham into the big, square salon, conscious of the questions trembling on his lips. 'Sorry about the mix-up,' she proffered over a shoulder. 'We must have gone in different directions.'

'How did Blake come into the picture?' he asked, following her.

'Coincidence, just as he said. He was visiting someone on the excavation site at the monastery.' She picked up a book lying on one of the small inlaid tables, glancing at the title without really taking in the words. 'Are you reading this?'

'I was flicking through it while I waited for you.' He reached out to put a hand on her arm, eyes revealing sudden concern as she flinched involuntarily. 'What is it, Donna? You seem jumpy.' He paused, his brows drawing together. 'Has something happened?'

Donna made herself smile and shake her head. 'Nothing untoward. We had lunch, that's all.'

'Like civilised people?'

She looked at him sharply. 'Cynicism isn't your style.'

'I know.' He sounded rueful. 'It's the uncertainty—it's getting me down. Surely it can't hurt to at least broach the subject.'

'As a matter of fact, I already have,' she said, trying

to be casual about it. 'He isn't being very co-operative.'

'Why? It's no skin off his nose. Not after all this time.' There was another pause, and a change of tone. 'He hasn't suggested you get back together again, has he?'

'No.' She could say that in all honesty, knowing the way Graham meant it. Blake's declaration of intent had covered here and now, not the future. He wanted her as a woman, not a wife—or that was the impression he had given. 'I told you it was the wrong time,' she added. 'We're just going to have to wait.'

'With what patience we can muster.' Graham drew her to him, resting his cheek against her hair. 'I love you, Donna. Just keep remembering that. I can make you happy.'

She believed him. He would make a dependable partner in every respect. But did she really want another husband? Maybe she was one of those people just not cut out for marriage at all. The problem was going to be convincing Graham of that.

The rest of the day was relatively uneventful. Graham stuck close when they ventured from the house again to visit the fortress of Sacsayhuanan high above the town. Excavations were under way here too. Graham spoke to one of the archaeologists in charge, to be told that years of exploration remained but money was short. Everything boiled down to funding in the end. With field workers to pay and equipment to buy, to say nothing of research facilities, finance was always a major issue. Having the Linden Foundation to back their own expedition provided a rare security.

Dinner was taken at the house again, with everyone warned of an early start for the following day's trip. Janine kept Blake firmly to herself throughout the meal, their conversation too low to be clearly audible down the other end of the table, although it didn't appear to be of a particularly personal nature. Whatever disruption of arrangements might have taken place, she seemed to have forgiven him, Donna thought cynically. But then wasn't that what Blake had said of her: the sense to know when not to complain. He certainly had to know her pretty well for that kind of assessment. She was dismayed by the sheer force of emotion that reflection elicited.

Rising at five-thirty was no real hardship to Donna. Her father had always been an early riser himself, and her habits had been formed to suit his. Showered and dressed in cords and shirt, she came back to the bedroom, to find Janine only just stirring.

'I'm not coming,' the latter imparted, rolling over with an arm across her eyes to shield them from the light. 'I've seen Machu Picchu already, and I can't stand crowds.' The arm came down again, grey-green eyes fixing Donna with a faintly threatening gaze. 'Just remember your place in the scheme of things out here, that's all. Following Blake Mitchell around isn't going to gain you anything in any direction!'

Want to bet? Donna was tempted to retort, but refrained. The truth would quieten the other down and afford some satisfaction, but it would also create the kind of complications she preferred to avoid. She picked up her sketching satchel and left without answering.

The rail-car left the Santa Ana station at seven. Donna sat with Edith Remington and across from Blake, who was deep in discussion with two of the other male members of the party. So far he had not elected to pay her any particular attention. Neither would he, she told herself wryly. Not now that other more pressing matters claimed his mind.

With the rainy season not so long behind them, the grassland and lower mountain slopes were still green and verdant, although the agaves and cacti round the edges of the fields signified the general dryness of the climate. Donna had read that the seasons were beginning to lose their definitive patterns here just as in other parts of the world. There had even been snow in Cuzco in mid-July during recent years. Warmth at night was going to be a must. It was some comfort to know their equipment included heat sheets of the kind used in space missions in case of need.

Arriving at the tiny Machu Picchu station beside the rushing brown river, they found Dodge minibuses waiting to take them up the steep switchback of a roadway, robbing the occasion of much of its adventurous appeal. Necessary, however, Donna was bound to concede when they reached the top. Walking up fifteen hundred feet of mountain would be no easy task in the rarefied atmosphere. Even though here they were a couple of thousand feet lower than Cuzco her lungs still ached.

The first sight of the modern hotel and terraced fields beyond was somewhat disappointing, but once through the medieval-looking entrance to the citadel itself they were straight into the land of the Incas. A carpet of grass underfoot deadened sound as they wandered among the ruined remains, while clouds hanging low over the sugar-loaf peak which towered ahead cast mystical shadows over the old stones. There were llamas and alpacas wandering freely in the main plaza, just as they might have done in the past.

With the rest of the party scattered, Donna found herself a perch against the great stone slab which could once have been a sacrificial altar, and brought all her skill to bear in trying to capture the monumental view over the valley far below, undisturbed by the curious stares of other tourists. She would have liked to walk the original Inca trail to the western gateway, but with only a bare couple of hours left before the return to Cuzco it was too risky an undertaking. A night at the hotel would have been a good idea, although it was doubtful if they would have found rooms without prior booking.

She had been working for some fifteen minutes when Blake came across her. 'You're no landscape artist,' he commented with typical bluntness, looking over her shoulder at what she was doing. 'Why waste your time?'

'Because it is *my* time at the moment,' she said, too well aware that what he said was true. 'And I feel like wasting it. Don't worry, when we get to Incanta I'll confine my efforts to whatever you deem necessary.'

'Good. A would-be Constable we can do without.' He lowered himself to a seat at her side, lifting a knee to rest a forearm comfortably across it. 'Unbelievable, isn't it? I envy Bingham what he must have felt when he first crawled up that mountainside and saw it.'

'It must have been quite a moment,' she agreed. Her pencil was still now, the mood destroyed. Damn Blake, she thought bitterly. Why couldn't he leave her alone!

'You'll survive,' he said, reading her thoughts the way he had so often done in the past. 'It's only a matter of time.'

Donna turned her head to look at him, a stray shaft of sunlight catching her hair as she did so and turning it to purest gold. She saw his eyes narrow suddenly with an expression she recognised of old, and felt her heart jerk as desire rose thick and swift within her. If only things were different. If only they could go back. Yet if they did she wouldn't now be sitting here seeing the things she was seeing, would have had no chance of doing the things she was going to be doing.

'Isn't it time you stopped fooling yourself?' she asked huskily. 'You've no more intention of making love to me than I have of letting you. What would the others think?'

'They wouldn't have to know,' he said. 'Even if they did it wouldn't be regarded with any great concern by most. Archaeologists are human too. If opportunity offers itself, few would refuse on the grounds of being above such mundane activities.'

'Opportunity isn't offering itself to you,' she pointed out. 'You're planning on taking it—at least, that's what you'd like me to believe.'

'Now why should I bother playing that kind of game?' His voice was low, his tone mocking. 'Remember when we were first married, how eager you used to be to make love? It didn't matter where or when, all you wanted was the sensation!'

Donna remembered all too clearly; remembered too that he had never been loth to indulge her. In that way if in no other they had been perfectly matched. But it hadn't been enough.

'You should never have married me,' she said. 'No matter what my motives were, yours hardly did you any justice.'

'I married you because I loved you,' he returned without emotion. 'Shortsighted of me, perhaps, considering I knew just how deep your feelings for me went, but I was willing to take a chance on your future development. I didn't count on the extent of your father's influence over you—or his jealousy.'

'Jealousy?' Her laugh jarred. 'Don't be ridiculous!'

'Oh, he was jealous all right. In every way but the physically intimate you'd taken your mother's place in his life. He couldn't stand the thought of you having any kind of feeling for another man.'

'You're wrong.' She was desperate to convince him. 'All he wanted was my happiness. If he'd felt the way you're saying he'd never have given us the opportunity to be alone together any time.'

'He had confidence in his hold on you. What he

forgot to make allowances for was sexual need.' He registered her expression with a twist of his lips. 'Don't look like that. You can no more help your nature than I can. Has your photographer friend been able to satisfy you?'

'I told you . . .' she said it between gritted teeth, hanging on to her control with everything she had '. . . we're not lovers.'

'That I find hard to believe. Not that it makes too much difference—he certainly won't be having you while I'm around.'

Donna gazed at him in silence for several seconds, unable to convince herself that he was playing games any longer. 'If you ever loved me,' she said at last, 'you'll stop trying to hurt me this way.'

'If I still loved you I wouldn't want to hurt you.' His mouth had a cruel line. 'And don't bother appealing to my better nature. I don't have one any more—not where you're concerned, at any rate.'

'Professor?' Juan Prieto, the Peruvian government representative, was standing on one of the lower terraces, speculation in his dark eyes as he looked up at the two of them. 'I am sorry to intrude, but I would like your opinion.'

'No problem. We've just finished our discussion.' Blake dropped down to join him, leaving Donna sitting alone on the cold bare rock.

She watched the two men move towards the Royal Tomb, the one tall and lean, the other small and swarthy. They might have finished their discussion for the moment, but she had to believe that Blake had meant every word he had said. Yet it took two, didn't it? He was hardly going to use force with all the team at close quarters. Ultimately the choice had to be hers. She only hoped she was going to have the strength of mind to make the right one.

Lunch was taken in the cafeteria-style dining room of the hotel, which was packed with visitors from all corners of the world. The Japanese were much in evidence, cameras at rest only while they ate. An Australian party at the next table were arguing the rival merits of bull and cock-fighting, both of which they had apparently seen down in Lima, while beyond a couple of Germans loudly proclaimed their prior right to seats taken from under their noses.

'At least we'll have Incanta to ourselves,' observed Edith Remington dryly, catching Donna's glance. 'You look a little subdued,' she added a moment later. 'Not coming down with mountain sickness, I hope?'

Donna shook her head, avoiding Blake's eyes. 'I'm fine, thanks.'

'That's good. It's been suggested that we have a last fling tonight, then spend tomorrow resting up ready for the journey. Juan knows a good place to eat out. He says there should be dancing too.' She laughed. 'You and Janine will have your work cut out keeping six men going!'

'Five,' corrected the man seated at her side, with whom Donna had only spoken a few words since her arrival. 'I'm too old for dancing at the best of times. At eleven thousand feet it's a fool's pastime!'

'Theo, you never even learned to dance.' Edith spoke with the familiarity of an old acquaintance. 'You had two left feet when you were twenty! I should know. I seemed to get landed with you at every University function. We took our degrees together,' she added somewhat unnecessarily for Donna's benefit. 'It seems a long time ago now.'

'It is a long time ago,' agreed her contemporary equably. 'There's a whole new generation come up after us—like Dr Mitchell here, and our two postgraduates,' nodding towards the other table where the two young men in question sat in earnest conversation with Juan Prieto. 'Overtaken in some cases.'

The latter remark was aimed though not barbed. Blake acknowledged it with a brief inclination of his head. 'I had all the breaks.'

'And took advantage of them.' The older man nodded sagely. 'You're not married, of course?'

Donna held her breath, sensing the fleeting glance Blake sent her way. 'I was once,' he said on a level note. 'She left me.'

'An occupational hazard. Mine did the same. Maybe I should have married you instead, Edith. We had more in common.'

'Marriage was never on my agenda.' The latter was looking at Blake, an odd expression in her eyes. 'You must have been badly hurt.'

He shrugged. 'Everything passes. We'd better be making tracks if we want to catch the train back.' His grin came easily. 'No pun intended!'

A blanket of fog had descended over the higher ground when they got outside, lending credence to the legend of the lost city. Without the sun the temperature felt decidedly chilly, and Donna for one was glad to board the rail-car and head for home.

It was almost seven by the time they reached the house. Janine was changing in the bedroom.

'Enjoy yourselves?' she asked carelessly as Donna closed the door.

'Yes.' There seemed little to add to that. She crossed the room to fish her suitcase down from the top of the locker where she had stored it, putting it down on the bed to extract the cream linen dress she had worn that first night in Lima. It was creased, but it would have to do. 'How was your day?' she added as an afterthought.

'Oh, I ended up going with Graham on his reconnaissance trip,' came the smooth reply. 'We'll have a tough time getting there, from the look of things. The whole landscape is wild. It's difficult enough to spot the site from the air, although Graham says his plates show a good outline. He certainly knows his job.'

'Of course.' Donna refused to be drawn. 'That's why he's here.' She hung the dress on a hanger, intending to take it into the bathroom with her where a little steam might drop out the worst of the creases. 'Incidentally, we're all supposed to be going out for a meal. Did you know?'

'Someone mentioned it as a possibility last night,' Janine answered. 'I've made my own arrangements.'

'With Blake?' The question was involuntary. Donna bit her lip, feeling the gaze swung in her direction.

'It it's any concern of yours, the answer is yes. We're old friends as well as colleagues.'

And I'm his wife! Donna wanted to shout, only it was too late for that. 'I think you might find he's changed his plans,' she said instead. 'I heard him tell Dr Remington he would be coming with the rest of us.'

Janine's mouth tightened, lending her features a certain hardness. 'Then you heard wrong.'

There was nothing else to be said to that. Donna took up the dress along with clean underwear and made for the bathroom, trying to tell herself she didn't care if Blake did spend the evening with Janine, and failing miserably. His relationship with the woman hardly tied in with his professed intentions towards her—unless he planned on taking advantage of them both. She wouldn't put that past him. These days she wouldn't put anything past him. He had become a totally different man from the one she had once known.

CHAPTER FOUR

JUAN Prieto's choice of a good place to spend an evening turned out to be a cross between restaurant and nightclub in one of the city's modern hotels. The nine of them took up two tables pushed together in one of the arched alcoves—a mixed bag, as Juan himself remarked. Certainly no other party in the place covered the same age range.

Donna kept her expression strictly neutral as she took her seat opposite Janine. Not that it was possible to gather, either from her face or from Blake's, whether any disagreement had occurred. As they were still sitting together the probability seemed unlikely. Donna had to admire Janine's fortitude. Faced with the same situation, she doubted if she herself could have shown the same lack of frustration.

Graham had been quiet throughout the journey. He was tired, he said now when Donna commented casually on the fact. The altitude was still affecting him adversely. She knew a few people never managed to make the adjustment, and worried in case he was one of them. Blake would have him replaced the moment he suspected that to be the case, and where would that leave her? His own interests aside, she needed Graham around to protect her from the assault Blake kept making on her senses. How self-centred could one get? she asked herself in rueful acknowledgment.

The meal was excellent, but she was in no mood to enjoy it. The sooner the expedition proper got under way, the better, she thought, listening to Janine monopolising the conversation. There was no denying

63

the woman's qualifications and expertise; if only she wasn't quite so full of her own brilliance. If it came right down to it, Blake could probably blind her with science, yet he made no attempt to push his own views even where, to Donna's certain knowledge, they differed. Unless those same views had altered radically in the last two years.

She was grateful when one of the postgraduates asked her to dance. At twenty-five, Michael Barratt was one of the most earnestly dedicated young men she had ever met. He wanted to talk about her father, she discovered when they were on the floor. He spoke the name with reverence.

'Professor Mitchell always refers to him as the major authority on the Inca civilisation,' he said. 'I heard him lecture a few times myself. You must be very proud to be his daughter.'

'I am,' Donna assured him. 'We were very close.'

'You never wanted to follow in his footsteps?'

'I didn't inherit his brain.' She had answered that same question so many times before, the words came automatically.

'Well, at least you're covering the same ground.' He smiled at his own mild joke, putting up a hand to push the heavily rimmed spectacles back up his nose for the umpteenth time. 'There should be plenty of work for you when we're on site.'

When? She was beginning to wonder if they would ever get there!

Graham was sitting alone at their end of the table when Michael returned her.

'I think I might take myself back to the house,' he said, looking anything but well.

'I'll come with you,' she offered, but he shook his head.

'I'd rather you didn't. Just say I was tired.' He smiled at her concern. 'Don't worry, I'll be okay. Juan tells me he's known people feel this way for days, then suddenly get over it. You're lucky it doesn't affect you the same.'

'It didn't the first time either,' she admitted. 'Not for more than a few hours, anyway. Are you sure you don't want me to come back with you?'

'Quite sure.' His tone lowered, smile twisting. 'Your husband might read things the wrong way.'

'Would it matter?' she asked with some deliberation. 'You want me to get that divorce, don't you?'

'Not that way. Mutual consent would be pleasanter.'

'Except that he hasn't consented. Not yet.' She summoned a smile. 'Time will tell. At least let me come with you to find a taxi.'

Reception telephoned for them, relaying the information that there would be a ten-minute delay. Donna insisted on sitting with Graham until the vehicle arrived outside the front entrance, accompanying him as far as the main doors to wave him off. She should have gone with him, she told herself as she turned back into the lobby; he looked so totally done in.

Blake met her at the door to the restaurant. 'I was just coming to look for you,' he said. 'What happened?'

Prevarication was a waste of time, Donna knew, yet she still attempted it. 'Graham didn't feel well— something he ate earlier, he thinks. He insisted I should stay.'

'Generous of him.' The grey eyes were not deceived. 'If he hasn't thrown it off by morning I'm going to have to do something about having him replaced. We're going to be a long way from medical aid where we're going.'

'You'd like that, wouldn't you?' she stated with asperity. 'You're just looking for an excuse to get rid of him!'

His expression didn't alter. 'It makes little difference where you're concerned. Shall we go back?'

Janine was watching the door as they came through. Skirting the edge of the dance floor, Donna knew a sudden urge to do something rash. 'Dance with me,' she said softly to Blake as they paused to let another couple pass. 'It's been a long time.'

He swung her out on to the floor without hesitation, holding her so that their bodies scarcely touched. 'Like this?' he asked sardonically. 'Or did you have something more intimate in mind?' He looked down at her when she failed to reply, lips thinning anew. 'Don't try using me to settle any scores. It could rebound on you.'

'I don't know what you mean,' she said.

'Yes, you do. You wanted to prove something to Janine.'

'Have you made love to her?' she demanded, driven by the need to hear him deny it.

'Yes,' he said quite calmly. 'Several times, as a matter of fact. Does that satisfy your curiosity?'

She was silent, assimilating the shock of having suspicion confirmed. She should have known he wouldn't bother to wrap it up.

'If you don't want to hear the truth don't ask the question,' he said after a moment or two. 'Did you really think I could go two years without a woman?'

'I doubt if you could go two weeks!' The words were torn from her. 'Anyway, she's welcome to you.'

'After I've finished with you.' He was openly mocking her. 'You've matured in some ways, Donna, if not in others. It's going to be interesting to find out just how far it goes.'

'Blake, stop it!' She was on the verge of pleading with him. 'Where's the point in it all?'

There was no softening of the lean features. 'The point in it all is that I want you. You could say I never stopped wanting you. It's a small enough price to pay for your freedom. You could even enjoy it if you let yourself. Physically we were good together. I'm sure we still shall be.' He brought her closer against him, making her conscious of every hard contour of his body. 'It's a pity we're all sharing rooms. We could make a night of it.'

'Why worry about it?' she said with scorn. 'Perhaps Janine wouldn't mind sharing your attentions.'

His hold on her tightened painfully. 'Janine and I have nothing going at the moment. This was to be Brinkman's party, remember?'

'Try telling her that!'

'I don't have to tell her anything. She has no more claim on my time than I have on hers.'

Perversely Donna felt a pang of sympathy for the other woman. Blake was as hard as nails. And whose fault was that? asked the small voice of conscience. He had given his trust once and had it thrown in his face. It was doubtful if he would risk that kind of hurt again.

For the first time she allowed herself to consider just what she had thrown away the day she had told him she was leaving him. Had she turned to him for comfort instead of her father, they might still have had a marriage. But what kind of marriage; that was the question. This way she had at least achieved a measure of independence.

Janine was talking to Theodore Newbould when they got back to the table. She ignored them both. Blake made no attempt to regain his seat.

'I don't know about the rest of you,' he announced, 'but I've had enough. Anybody who wants to stay on a while feel free. The bill's been paid.'

Apparently nobody did. Donna dropped back to walk alongside Edith Remington as they all made their way from the place, feeling the older woman's discerning glance.

'Tell me to mind my own business, if you like,' she said, 'but you and Blake Mitchell have met before, haven't you?'

That was one way of putting it, Donna thought without humour. Aloud she said wryly, 'Is it that obvious?'

'Only in a certain atmosphere between the two of you whenever you come into contact.' Edith paused. 'Not a happy relationship, I gather?'

'It's a long story.'

'That's all right. I'm not asking for details.' Her tone was dry. 'Just keep a sharp eye open for our Dr Meade. She already has him marked down as her property. If she can get you dropped from the team she'll do it, believe me. I've seen her type of self-interest before.'

Except that she might not find it so easy a task when Blake himself wanted her here, reflected Donna. It would be interesting to see what might happen should she do something, or appear to do something, which would merit her being thrown off the team.

'She doesn't have much time left,' she said aloud. 'Once we leave for Incanta I'm safe enough.'

'Always providing you don't fall and break an ankle like poor old John Brinkman. It's easy to trip up in the kind of country we'll be travelling through.'

Edith said no more after that, leaving Donna with food for thought. Not that she really believed the implication. Janine might be full of herself, and possessive over Blake, but to see her as any kind of physical threat was surely beyond reason. Edith was allowing her imagination to run away with her. Even scientists could make mistakes in judgment.

Whether by accident or design, the journey back to the house found her seated beside Blake in the taxi with Janine on his other side. The pressure of his thigh against hers was no accident, though, of that she was sure. In all probability he was applying the same tactic to Janine, and laughing to himself at the situation.

Janine said something to him softly before they got out of the taxi, and he replied equally quietly. Donna stalked ahead of them into the house, trying to keep her feelings to herself as she saw Edith Remington watching her. No one seemed inclined to linger up. Donna asked Theo to check on Graham, who was occupying the same room, to be told that the latter was sleeping and seemed comfortable enough. With any luck he would be over the worst of the symptoms when he woke in the morning.

Janine had nothing at all to say as the two of them prepared for bed, and Donna saw no reason to break the silence herself. The thought of spending several weeks sharing a tent with the archaeologist was a depressing one, yet there seemed no way out of it. Nothing about this job was turning out the way she had hoped, and she could hardly lay the whole of the blame at Blake's door. She needed to get things into perspective again.

She slept eventually, awakening what could have been hours or merely minutes later to find the other bed empty. It had been the sound of the door closing softly which had awoken her. Remembering those last whispered words from Blake, she thought she knew where Janine was headed. An assignation, no less!

Resentment, mingled with some other emotion, stirred her into action. She had to know if it was true. What difference it was going to make she didn't stop to consider.

The house seemed quiet enough, although lights still burned both upstairs and down. Donna descended step by step, clutching her wrap about her as she peered over the carved balustrade into the empty hallway. There was no one there—nor in the salon either. The dining salon was along the passageway, which itself gave on to a small, enclosed patio. Other doors led to rooms she had not yet seen.

Even as she stood there, irresolute, facing the possibility that she had been wrong, one of the latter opened and Blake came out. He halted abruptly when he saw her.

'Looking for me?' he asked.

'Yes. No!' She hardly knew what she was saying, her confusion was so great. He was still fully dressed. 'I thought I heard a noise,' she tagged on lamely.

'From upstairs?' He sounded sceptical. 'Nothing I've been doing could have penetrated that far.'

'What have you been doing?' The question had to be asked.

By way of answer, he took a step backwards into the room again and beckoned her after him. She followed because she couldn't help herself, to find what appeared to be a cross between study and small library. There was no one else present, that was immediately apparent.

'Satisfied?' Blake asked on a mocking note, and she realised he knew exactly what was in her mind. 'You wouldn't like to look behind the shutters?'

'I heard a noise,' she repeated stubbornly. 'That's all. I'll go back to bed now.'

'You asked me what I'd been doing.' He was somehow behind her and closing the door, trapping her in the room. 'A question that deserves an answer.' A movement of his hand indicated the heavy desk on which rested a scattering of photographs and other paperwork. 'I've been studying the air-shots, among other things. There's a lot to be gleaned from a good air photograph. They show features that can be completely invisible from the ground—or am I preaching to the initiated?'

'I know the value,' she said. 'You'll admit Graham knows his job, then?'

'I never denied it. He wouldn't be here at all if he didn't. These are good and clear. I've already learned a great deal. For instance, the outline drawn up by the previous party is nowhere near complete.' They were across at the desk now, his finger stabbing one of the plates. 'See that shadow there against the mountain—the way it follows a different line? There could be more ruins covered by undergrowth, which would make the whole site a piece larger than we imagined. It could be just a military stronghold as was suggested, but I've a strong feeling we're going to make some important finds once we get dug in. We're lucky in being able to call on the Quechua for labour. There's a sizeable village where we're due to leave the cars.'

'Yes, I know.' Donna was vibrantly aware of the closeness of the lean, muscular body, of the weight of the hand resting on her shoulder. 'How long will it take us to get there?'

'To the village? A day if we're lucky. The roads aren't good. After that it depends entirely on what we find. From the look of things it isn't going to be an easy trek.'

'That's what Janine said.' She used the name deliberately, waiting for his reaction and tensing in unison.

'Are you going to keep throwing her in my face?' Blake growled softly. 'I told you it was all over between us. We're colleagues, nothing else.'

'Does she know that?'

'She should.' The hand on her shoulder tightened its grip as she started to move, holding her securely. 'Not so fast! Is that why you came down—hoping to find us together?'

'She left the room,' said Donna, keeping her face turned from his. 'I was curious, that's all.'

'Not jealous, by any chance?' The question was jeering. 'I don't suppose it would have occurred to you that she might have gone to the bathroom? Now you're going to be missing and she's going to be doing the wondering.'

'In which case I'd better be getting back.' She made another attempt to free herself, twisting under his fingers as he slid them around the back of her neck. 'Blake, let me go!'

'Not on your life,' he said. 'This is where you start paying, Donna. And you brought it on yourself.'

There was no fighting him, because he already had her head held fast with both hands about her throat. Response leapt in her the moment his lips touched hers, tremor after tremor running through her body with nothing she could do to stop them. He made no attempt to force anything on her, his mouth questing rather than taking, easing her lips open by gradual degrees as her willpower ebbed.

Her wrap came open to a single tug of his fingers, the pullover-style pyjama top giving him pause only for a moment. The hand sliding up to cover her breast moved in exploratory fashion, fingers sensitive. She quivered to his touch, no longer resisting the emotions coursing through her. This man was her husband, and she wanted him. That was as far as she allowed her thoughts to go.

The carpet cushioned her descending weight. Blake came down at her side, pulling up the pyjama top to bare both her breasts to his lips, delicately tracing one pale aureole with the tip of his tongue before closing the very edges of his teeth about her hardened nipple. If there had been any faint desire left in her to stop him, it was gone now, her senses alive to the memory of total fulfilment. How could she have ever walked away from this? she wondered, tremoring to the intimate touch of his hands. It was all that made life worth living! She said his name deep and low in her throat.

He was breathing heavily when he lifted his head from her, eyes narrowed with the effort of control. 'How does it feel to want something you can't have?' he asked on a cruel note. 'Tell me how it feels.'

'Blake, no!' Her throat hurt, the sound itself full of pain. 'You can't do this to me!'

'Why not? You did it to me.'

'Not this way.'

'No, worse. You stripped me of everything. Six months, that was all you allowed me.' His voice was low and rough. 'You've still no concept of what you put me through, have you? I loved you, you little bitch!'

'I'm sorry.' It was the only thing she could say. She hadn't loved him. Not in any way he could accept. He had wanted her heart and soul; she had given him her body—and that only for a limited time.

'It's a start.' He eased himself away from her, looking down at her slender curving shape with cynicism. 'I'm fighting a strong urge to say to hell with it and take you now, only I know I'd regret it afterwards. You need to suffer a little more first.'

'There won't be a next time,' she said tautly as he got to his feet. 'I'll make sure there isn't!'

He bent down and hauled her to a standing position before she could draw breath to protest, using his free hand to adjust her clothing. 'You'd better get back to bed, before someone comes looking for you.'

'If you mean Janine Meade, perhaps she should know the truth,' Donna jerked out.

His shrug was indifferent. 'What you choose to tell her, or anyone else for that matter, is entirely up to you. I don't give a damn one way or another. Whichever way, you'll take what's coming to you.'

'Not if I leave the team right here in Cuzco.'

'And forfeit the prestige of working on the Incanta dig?' He shook his head. 'You won't do that, Donna. Not if you want to make anything of a career for yourself.'

'I hate you, Blake!' The words were impassioned, blue eyes fired with it.

'I know.' His smile mocked her anger. 'But you don't hate what I can do to you, and that's the only emotion of yours I'm interested in. Now go on back to bed, I have to clear up in here.'

She left him to it, standing for a moment in the corridor outside to gather herself together. She had said she hated him, but that wasn't strictly true. The emotions he aroused in her were far more complex than that. She had caused him pain and anguish two years ago; could she blame him too much now for wanting to put her through a little of the same? It was what was to happen afterwards that was beginning to matter the most.

Janine sat up in bed as she slipped into the room, face set like a mask. 'Where the hell have you been?' she demanded.

If there was ever a moment for telling the plain and simple truth that moment was now, but Donna couldn't bring herself to take it. Her marriage was her own affair, not something to be conjectured about by anyone else. 'Minding my own business,' she said coolly. 'Supposing you do the same?'

Janine drew in a sharp breath. 'Don't you dare speak to me like that! I'll have you thrown off the team!'

'You can't.' Donna took off her wrap to slide between the sheets. 'Not unless you can persuade Professor Mitchell to get rid of me.'

'Is he the one you've been with?'

'I told you, it's none of your business.' She was

being deliberately provocative, Donna knew, but she no longer cared. Too much had happened tonight for her to take any more from a woman she didn't even like. She turned over to face the wall and resolutely closed her eyes. 'If you don't mind, I'd like to go to sleep.'

It was not a restful night. Awakening from a fitful doze around seven, Donna found she was not the only one who had been unable to sleep. Janine's bed was empty, the covers thrown back in obvious abandonment. Memory of the previous night's altercation brought a feeling of shame. There had been other, less inciting ways to handle the question of her absence. What she had said was likely to cause trouble of the kind best avoided.

There was still no sign of Janine when she went down to the salon before breakfast, but Graham was already down. He looked better, Donna thought in relief.

His first words confirmed her diagnosis. The headaches were gone, along with the dizziness, he said. Just a matter of time, as Juan had intimated.

'We'll not be moving far today,' he added. 'Blake wants everybody to stick close and rest up.'

'You've seen him?' She was hard put to it to keep her tone neutral.

'He's in one of the other rooms down there discussing the aerial views I took yesterday with Janine. I left them to it. I'd contributed all I had to say on the subject.' He was watching her with thoughtfully drawn brows. 'I never got round to asking you last night, but how did the trip go?'

'Much as you might expect,' she said. 'There were too many people. At least they're not likely to turn Incanta into a regular tourist attraction. It would cost too much to run a road through, if the country is anything like it looks from those photographs you took.'

'You've seen them?' There was an odd note in his voice. 'When?'

'Last night after we got back.' She looked up in relief as Edith came into the room. 'Good morning. By this time tomorrow we should be on our way!'

'And none too soon,' agreed the other. 'I'm itching to get back to work!'

They were all at breakfast before Blake and Janine joined them. Donna studiously avoided catching either pair of eyes, concentrating on her plate and on Graham at her side. If Janine had confronted Blake about last night she would know about it soon enough, although what he might have told her was open to doubt.

The party broke up after the meal, with the men going off to supervise the loading of precious equipment into the three Land Rovers. With her own personal gear still to sort, Donna went up to the bedroom to make a start, laying everything out on the bed before attempting to pack the waterproof canvas rucksack she would be carrying herself once they left the cars. Janine found her there.

'Blake is going to have a word with you later,' she said from the doorway on a note of satisfaction. 'He agrees that I merit a little more respect than you seem prepared to grant me.'

'I respect your qualifications,' Donna returned without looking round. 'But that doesn't give you any right to ask me personal questions. At any rate, I'm not obliged to answer them.'

'Especially when you're smarting from a put-down such as you had last night.'

'Is that what I had?' Donna still refused to turn.

'Don't prevaricate for me. Do you think a man like Blake Mitchell is going to bother with a little nobody like you? Oh, yes, I know all about your father. He's the only reason you got this job in the first place. John

Brinkman may have been impressed by the name, but I'm not. Your father's dead. His work will be surpassed by others.'

'You among them, I imagine?'

'Why not? I'm starting where he left off. So is Blake. We work well together, he and I.'

'Good for you.' Donna would dearly have liked to know exactly what Blake had told her about the previous night, but she was not about to ask. There would be no further opportunity for him to try the same tactics again. Not at Incanta. If he wanted her so much he should have taken her while he had the chance. She shut out the part of her that wished he had.

Having said all she had come to say, Janine departed again. Struggling with the stiff leather strap holding down one front flap of her rucksack, Donna wondered blindly why she was going on. The simplest way out would be to pack her suitcase and take the afternoon flight down to Lima.

Except how would she explain to Graham? Telling him the truth would only complicate matters further. No, she had to see it through. There was no other way.

CHAPTER FIVE

THE household was roused at five to a morning not yet under way. Shivering in the unheated bedroom, Donna clothed herself in the cord trousers and brushed cotton shirt which were to see her through the day, too well aware that evening would find them all in conditions far removed from those they had enjoyed for the past few days.

Janine was quiet; she seemed preoccupied. Planning ahead, Donna surmised. There would be little time for anything outside of the job itself in the weeks to come.

Breakfast was good and substantial, although few of them felt like eating very much at that hour. By the time they were ready to leave the sun was up, but it was still cool enough to make anoraks a necessity. They found the loaded Land Rovers ready and waiting, driven by Indians wearing European-style clothing. They all spoke English, Blake had said, though with varying degrees of fluency. Looking at the inexpressive, lined brown countenance of her own driver, Donna doubted if verbal communication was high on his list of essential functions.

She was to travel in the second of the three vehicles, along with Graham and Michael Barratt; Blake, Janine and Juan Prieto being in the lead. The second of the two postgraduates, Philip Hardy, brought up the rear alongside Edith and Theo Newbould. He and Michael were scheduled to spend a matter of only two or three weeks out at the site before returning to their formal studies—an opportunity fully appreciated by both young men. If things got on top of her, Donna told herself with irony, she could always return with them.

78

They took the Anta road from Cuzco, following the railway as far as the village of Cachimayo, then branching off for Chinchero where they would leave the better-used road behind. Already stiff, Donna was glad to take the opportunity to stretch her legs when they reached the latter place, and view the magnificent frescoes in the church. Coming out again into the sparkling air, they found time to walk among the market stalls in the square and listen to the local women in their black skirts and red mantas, operating a barter system of trade with others wearing distinctive tall white hats. Here again there was little sense of the passage of time.

Faced with the extra thousand or so feet of altitude, Graham was obviously finding any kind of exertion difficult. Donna saw Blake glance at him sharply once or twice, and knew concern herself. People had been known to suffer embolisms at these heights. It was a relief to find the dirt road which took them on the next stage of the journey dropping fairly rapidly to more comfortable levels; to hear his breathing ease. Incanta should be safe enough at a little above eight thousand feet. It was just a matter of getting there.

'Stop worrying about me,' he murmured when she exposed her feelings at one point. 'I'll be okay.' He attempted a laugh, finding even that minor exertion something of a strain. 'And I always prided myself on being fit!'

'Perhaps we should all have had medicals before coming on the expedition,' suggested Michael Barratt seriously. 'Being ill where we're going could be a bad business.'

'Being ill anywhere is a bad business,' returned the other man shortly. 'Leave it alone, will you. *Both* of you!'

Donna ignored the terseness, recognising its cause,

but Michael was obviously affronted. He didn't speak for several kilometres.

The journey was long but never tedious. In the valleys the scenery was softer, with fields of maize clinging to the hillsides like so many postage stamps above the primitive villages, but always ahead lay the towering, snow-capped peaks of the *cordillera*, magnificent in sunlight. As predicted, the road surface left a lot to be desired. All three vehicles remained as close as could be managed within the limits of practicality in case of breakdown. Being stranded in this kind of country was not an experience to be taken lightly.

It was almost sundown before they finally reached their destination for the night. Viewing the scattering of roughly thatched houses, Donna wondered how someone like Janine managed to reconcile her obvious concern with appearances, with the shortcomings of most field situations. The only running water both here and at Incanta would come from the river, while toilet facilities could at best be described as makeshift. One thing was certain, hot baths were going to be a thing of the past. A bowl of warm water would be the best any of them could hope for.

The inhabitants of the village themselves proved friendly enough, supplying the party with an empty earth-floored hut among the nine of them against the chill of the coming night, and offering quantities of the region's wild potato in exchange for dried milk and egg from supplies. Life here was hard, yet smiles were abundant. The children showed the same curiosity as those from other parts of the globe, watching with open-mouthed wonder as preparations were made for a meal to be cooked on the portable stove. It was only now Donna realised that their drivers had more than one function, a rota system having apparently been agreed between two of them. When it came down to organisation, this whole expedition had to have been handled by an expert. Whoever he was, he had left nothing to chance.

The party ate together in the bare room allocated, squatting on the floor in the absence of chairs. Cooked Peruvian style, the chicken tasted strongly of pimentos but was good and filling. From here on in they would be living mostly out of tins and packets, Donna surmised, which meant there had to be a fairly regular delivery to the site considering the limitations in carrying capacity of the three Land Rovers.

'Helicopter,' Edith Remington supplied when she mentioned the point. 'The first thing we have to establish when we reach the site is a landing zone. Shouldn't be too difficult. There's a whole reel of foot-wide tape to use for markers.' She paused to stab a piece of chicken with her fork, adding on an ironical note, 'Starting to get cold feet?'

'No more than any other bit,' Donna responded wryly. 'My blood must be thin.'

'You need a man to keep you warm,' said Edith, not bothering to keep her voice down. 'You've plenty of choice.'

'Not while I'm around.' Blake sounded deceptively lazy. 'There'll be enough exercise on site to keep everybody glowing.'

Donna met the grey eyes with an equilibrium she was far from feeling. 'Drawing is a static art—unless you intend everybody should grab a spade and start digging!'

'We'll all of us do whatever's necessary,' came the unmoved response. 'Not that "grabbing a spade" strikes a very professional note.'

'A figure of speech,' she said, denying him the pleasure of seeing her discomfited. 'My father left me his very own trowel.'

'Which you'll hardly be using,' Janine cut in smoothly. 'You're only here to record our finds.'

'But without accurate records any excavation is a waste of time,' said Edith, still poking at her chicken. 'We all know that.'

That the younger woman had registered the unspoken criticism was obvious from the line of her mouth, but she made no reply, turning away to speak to Blake.

'Thanks,' offered Donna sotto voce.

'Nothing to thank me for,' the anthropologist denied. 'I was only stating the truth. I daresay we could all do our own recording if it came to it, but apart from the time, I can't draw for peanuts. If the results of this dig of ours are ever going to be published we've dire need of both you and Graham over there, so don't let anyone tell you different.'

Graham had barely touched his food, Donna noted, looking across to where he sat propped against the mud brick wall. When he got up and left the hut, she gave him a few minutes before following, finding him standing with hands thrust deep into his anorak pockets as he contemplated the cool clear night.

'I'm okay,' he insisted when she posed the question. 'So I still get breathless. I'm not on my own there.'

'You didn't eat,' she said hesitantly. 'I thought . . .'

'I don't care for chicken at the best of times. Tonight's wasn't exactly tempting.' He turned his head to glance her way, his expression difficult to decipher in the darkness. 'What is it with you and that husband of yours?'

'I'm not sure what you mean.' Even to her own ears her voice held no conviction.

'Don't try to fool me, Donna. You still feel something for him, don't you?' He waited for an answer, his lips thinning when none was forthcoming. 'Enough to go back to him?'

'He hasn't asked me to go back to him.'

'That doesn't answer the question.'

She shrugged, trying to be honest about it. 'I don't even know him any more—if I ever did. I'm not sure what I feel.'

'But he stirs something in you I've never managed to reach.' Graham's tone was flat. 'I think we'd better call it a day, don't you.' It was a statement, not a question.

'No!' There was alarm in her voice. 'Graham, I need you!'

'For what? Protection against your own instincts?' He shook his head. 'No way, Donna. I don't have that generous a spirit. You've already made up your mind you're not going to marry me—I can sense it in you.'

She could hardly deny it. She looked back at him ruefully. 'I feel so mixed up about everything.'

'About Blake maybe, not about us. It's over. That's final. From now on we'll just be part of the team.'

'Can't we even be friends?' she ventured, and saw his mouth slant.

'We shan't be enemies, if that's what you mean. We both have a job to do. Let's leave it at that.' He started to move back towards the hut, pausing when she remained motionless to look back at her. 'It's okay. You don't have to do any worrying over me—not in any sense. Just concentrate on straightening out your own life.'

Which was easier said than done, Donna acknowledged hollowly, going after him. Where Blake was concerned nothing was clear-cut.

With nine of them sleeping in the one hut space was limited to a few feet each. Aside from divesting themselves of anoraks and footwear, nobody attempted to undress for the night, sliding into their respective sleeping bags as they were. The atmosphere was claustrophobic, but they were all of them too weary to care. Janine had managed to place herself at Blake's side, Donna noted before she pulled up the zip on her own padded bag. Not that it was going to do her much good in the circumstances. Even Blake would draw the line at conducting any kind of liaison in company.

Graham had elected to sleep on the far side of the hut between Theo and Michael. If anyone had noticed the rift between them nothing had been said. There was an empty feeling deep down inside Donna. In Graham she had lost a good man—and for what? Blake was refusing to consider divorce right now, but it might be another story when they got back home. No matter what happened between then and now, they had no future together.

First light was just beginning to streak the sky beyond the open doorway when she awoke. No one else was stirring yet; she could hear the sound of steady breathing from all points of the room. The morning air struck cold on the exposed skin of her face, dispelling the last remnants of sleep. Faced with a choice between lying there with only her thoughts for company for the next hour or so or getting up, she chose the latter, crawling from the sleeping bag to step gingerly over recumbent bodies to reach the doorway where she could pull on her lightweight walking boots without disturbing anyone.

The village lay on a small cleared plateau overlooking a forested ravine. Beyond lay wooded slopes and the ever-present backcloth of the *cordillera*, just coming into view behind a sky turning crimson from the east as distant layers of cloud caught the rays of a sun still well below the horizon. Sitting with her back against a rock, Donna watched and waited, oblivious to the chill as fresh features of the landscape were slowly revealed to her. Civilisation seemed a million miles away.

The scrape of a boot on rock jerked her out of the

trance. When she turned her head Blake was standing a few feet away.

'I heard you leave the hut,' he said. 'When you didn't come back after ten minutes I thought something had happened to you. Aren't you cold sitting here?'

'No,' she denied. 'At least, not unduly. I'm waiting for the sun to rise.'

'It's going to be another half hour before that happens. You'd better get back in the warmth.'

'No!' She said it fiercely through her teeth, without raising her voice above a whisper. 'Just leave me alone, Blake. I'm not your responsibility!'

'Like it or not, that's exactly what you are.' His own tone was clipped. 'Do you want me to carry you back?'

'I *want* you to leave me alone.' Knees drawn up against her chest, she glared at him, willing herself not to shiver in the chill air. 'Can't you understand? I don't want you near me!'

'That would be unfortunate,' he said, 'if it were true.' With one swift movement he leaned down and grabbed a wrist, yanking her to her feet, the anger in him transmitting itself via the contact. 'Now come on back to the hut.'

The strength with which she tore her arm free of his grasp took them both by surprise. With no thought beyond the immediate one of getting away from him, Donna sprang into motion, running across the slope. It must have rained a little during the night, she realised, feeling the ground start to slide beneath her feet. She was dangerously close to the plateau edge where the rock fell sheer into the ravine. She scrabbled to retain her footing but found herself suddenly down on her knees and still sliding, her hands shooting out in panic to grab at any projection offering itself.

She was almost at the edge before Blake reached her. He had cut down at an angle across firmer ground and come in from below. Holding her grimly, he drew her on to secure land again, and from there back up to where they had started, breathing heavily with the strain as he jerked her roughly upright.

'You little fool!' he gritted. 'Are you trying to kill yourself?'

'I wouldn't have fallen if the ground had been dry,' she replied, fighting for her own breath. 'It's supposed to be the dry season! How was I to know it had rained?'

'The dry season doesn't mean no rain ever falls,' he said in the manner of one explaining to a child, 'it means it seldom falls. Last night's lasted about two minutes, if that. Just enough to make conditions treacherous for the unwary. Where the devil did you think you were going anyway?'

'Anywhere you weren't,' she responded smartly, recovering by the second. 'If I had gone over it would have been directly your fault!'

She was hard against him before she could say anything else, his mouth covering hers with brutal insistence. She felt his arm slide under her knees and was lifted from the ground, her breath still trapped by the relentless pressure. The nearest hut had a door hung on crude animal skin hinges—a store, Donna remembered thinking on last night's brief tour of the village. Only food had any real value out here.

Supposition was proved right when Blake dumped her down on a bed of dried maize, kicking the door to behind him with a well-aimed foot. It was dark and airless, with no window to relieve either condition. Maize made anything but a comfortable bed, grains of it infiltrating everywhere. The dust went up her nose, making her want to sneeze—except that sneezing was totally impossible while Blake was still kissing her, his body weight pressing her further and further down into the shifting pile. There was heat in the deeper layers, striking a responsive chord in her as she felt his fingers at her waistband. He couldn't! Not in here. Suppose someone came and found them rolling around naked in their precious grain?

She stopped struggling abruptly with the material halfway over her hips, head cocked in a listening attitude. 'Blake,' she said with new urgency, 'I think there are rats in here!'

It stopped him, if only for a moment. She could see the paler blur of his face bending over her, the movement as he turned an ear to listen. The rustling came again right on cue, the location a mere few feet away. Something was ferreting around in the grain, that was obvious. Donna had never seen an Andean rat and didn't much want to do so now. She clutched desperately at his sleeve.

'Get me out of here! Please, Blake, get me out!'

'Whatever it is we're not what it's interested in,' he said without attempting to get up.

'Then think of the villagers,' she hissed. 'Do you think it's fair to contaminate their food supplies?'

His laugh came low. 'With rats and lord knows what else loose in the grain I doubt if a few human microbes are going to make much difference. Still, you may have a point. There'll be other opportunities.'

Donna sat up as he rolled away from her, tugging her clothing back into place with fingers that trembled. Blake had never had any real intention of taking her in this place; he had simply been playing with her.

'If I agreed to let you make love to me just once for old times' sake, would you leave me alone after that?' she asked, and scarcely knew what she wanted the answer to be.

It wasn't immediately forthcoming. Blake seemed to be considering. When he did speak his tone left her in little doubt of his feelings. 'When we do make love it won't be a case of *letting* me do anything. You'll want it the same way I will.'

She wanted him now, she was bound to acknowledge the fact. Her body ached with the need to be back in those warm, safe arms of his. Only she'd be damned if she would ever let him know it again. Not after last night. All he wanted was revenge.

The sun was just lifting itself over the rim of the world when they got outside, warming the landscape with its fast spreading rays. Already the village was astir. Eyes watched their progress across the rough stone pathway to their own hut.

'Been for an early morning jog?' asked Theo Newbould mildly when they went inside. He was the only one fully awake, sitting up with his feet still buried in the sleeping bag and his back against a wall. 'I contemplated coming to join you, but age got the better part of valour. How was the sunrise?'

'An experience,' Donna told him dryly. 'I think they've got the stove going out back already. Perhaps we should start waking the others.'

Preparing for the day within the confines of their surrounding was an experience in itself. With hot water at a premium, most of them had to be content with a lick and a promise by way of a wash, although Janine managed to secure enough in her bowl to have some left over for washing out minor items of clothing. Wrapped in a towel, and carried along the top of her backpack, these would most likely be dry and ready to wear again by the time they reached their destination. Faced with more than thirty kilometres of hard walking it was more than possible that they wouldn't make Incanta in one day, Donna knew. Tonight they would sleep where opportunity offered itself.

Hollow-eyed and obviously feeling less than well, Graham made every attempt to throw himself into preparations for departure with good spirit, ignoring Donna's entreaty to take it easy. In the end it was Blake who called a halt.

'I'm sorry,' he said to the younger man, 'but I'm sending you back with the returning car for further acclimatisation. If you recover you can come out on the first supply trip in about a week.'

'I can pick up at Incanta,' Graham protested. 'It's lower than this.'

'After a thirty-kilometre hike touching twelve thousand?' Blake shook his head. 'It's scheduled to tax the best of us. It would finish you. A week's rest might do the trick.'

'And if it doesn't?'

The shrug told its own story. 'I'll cover that when I come to it.'

There was no arguing with him. Graham turned away without another word and moved his gear over to the waiting Land Rover. Donna went after him.

'I hate this,' she said. 'Especially now. I wish there was something I could do to help.'

The smile he gave her held an odd kind of acceptance. 'There's nothing anyone can do. As a matter of fact, Blake's quite right—I don't belong here.'

She looked at him in bewilderment. 'I don't know what you mean.'

'Simply that I went to see a medic the morning you went to Macchu Picchu and he told me to go on home.' He shook his head at her look of concern. 'No, it isn't life or death, but it could possibly be dangerous to overstrain myself. Apparently I have a heart murmur. At normal altitudes it's unlikely to give me any trouble for a long time to come, but up here it's a different story.'

'Why didn't you tell me before?' she whispered. '*Why*, Graham?'

'Because there were a lot of things I wasn't ready to give up,' he said flatly. 'The tablets I had prescribed for me seemed to help a bit at first, only the effects don't last long. I shan't be coming back, Donna. I'll take steps to secure a reputable replacement before heading home.' He hesitated, his glance going beyond her shoulder to the spot where Blake and the others were busy sorting loads for the Quechua pack animals. 'Just keep that to yourself for a little while, though, will you?'

'Of course.' She didn't fully understand his reasoning, but she was more than willing to go along with anything he asked of her. Guilt lay thick in her throat. 'Graham, let me come back with you. We can start again.'

He shook his head again, expression resigned. 'It wouldn't be any use. You're still in love with Blake.'

'No!' The force of the denial was as much for her own sake as for his. 'I despise him!'

'You despise yourself more for having given him up in the first place. He's going to be a harder nut to crack this time, but you'll do it if you set your mind to it.' He leaned down suddenly and kissed her on the lips. 'That's for what we shared. It isn't your fault it wasn't enough.'

He was in the front passenger seat before she could say anything, lifting a hand in smiling farewell as the driver put the vehicle into motion. 'See you some time.'

Donna made no attempt to conceal the tears in her eyes as she went back to work with the rest of the party. Blake looked at her with cynicism but kept his own counsel. It was left to Edith to offer the only genuine sympathy available.

'He'll be back,' she said. 'And all the better for it. In the meantime, start thinking about climbing a couple of thousand feet over that pass. We're all going to need what breath we have!'

The party was ready to leave by eight, with the heavier equipment safely packed on the backs of the woolly-coated llamas belonging to their Indian guides and helpers. The fees paid to the villagers for their services would keep the whole place going for a year, Blake had advised the previous evening, which explained the apparent lack of concern on behalf of those left behind by those due to spend the coming few weeks digging in the hills.

Strung out along the rocky trail as they left the village they made a strange sight, Donna thought. It would be eight weeks or more before she saw the place again. She was thankful for the long-range radio which would keep them in touch with home base. To be totally cut off in this kind of terrain was inadvisable. People had been known to die from relatively minor ailments simply because medical aid couldn't be summoned in time. That knowledge alone was sobering.

CHAPTER SIX

LUNCHTIME found them on the edge of the tough yellow grassland called *puna* at around twelve thousand feet, with the snowline still another four thousand feet above and several kilometres to the north west. Although cold in the shade, the air was warm enough in sunlight to make anoraks unnecessary. Breathing at this height was painful, each intake an effort. Donna felt as if her heart was bouncing around inside her ribs like a piece of loose machinery. She envied the Indians, whose barrel-like chests enclosed lungs of infinite capacity. Born and bred in the mountains, they could exert themselves all day without ill-effect.

Edith appeared to be suffering too, although strenuously denying the fact.

'My heart is as strong as an ox,' she claimed when they paused to eat beside a mountain stream. 'Otherwise I shouldn't have contemplated making the trip.'

'Wouldn't it have been easier in the long run to ferry the whole party in by helicopter?' ventured Donna, sensing the answer even before it was forthcoming.

'Complete with supplies? That would have taken a couple of dozen trips. Anyway, this is good experience. We'll be coming into Incanta via the old Inca roadway, where it still exists—or so we're led to believe from our predecessors' account.'

'Not too reliable,' put in Blake, overhearing the latter remark. 'They were little more than amateurs. It's doubtful if they were on site long enough to do any damage, thank heaven.' His eyes were on Donna. 'How do you feel?'

'Well enough to continue,' she responded stiffly. 'You can't send the whole team back to base.'

'It hadn't occurred to me to think about sending you back,' he said without any change of tone. 'Call it a solicitous enquiry. We'll be moving out in ten minutes. I want to be well down the mountain by nightfall.'

'You two should be married,' murmured Edith as he moved away. She viewed Donna's startled expression with a bland little smile. 'Or should I say reconciled?'

It took Donna a moment or two to adjust, her teeth biting into her lower lip. 'How did you know?' she asked at length.

'It came to me the other day at Machu Picchu when he said he'd once been married, although I had to tease my memory for the source. It was a snippet in some publication or other a couple of years ago when he returned from England after working with your father. I'd had the two names tied together in my mind from the start without realising why. Watching the two of you this last couple of days confirmed the theory.' She shook her head. 'Don't worry, I shan't go blabbing it around. Whatever sorting out you've to do it's between the two of you. Not that I envy you the task. He's a hard man.'

'He wasn't always,' Donna said softly. 'At least, not in the same way.' Her eyes followed the tall figure moving across the stone track to where Janine sat with Michael and Philip. 'It was a shock to us both to meet up in Lima the way we did. We're still learning to cope with it.'

'It takes time,' Edith agreed. 'Our Dr Meade doesn't help. You realise she's after him for herself?'

'She can have him.' Donna's tone had gone flat, her eyes losing their brilliance. 'I suppose we'd better start getting ourselves together. At least from here it's all downhill!'

Conditions became easier during the course of the afternoon. By four o'clock they had covered nineteen of the thirty kilometres and found shelter for the night in a narrow valley where the remains of a stone-surfaced roadway were still very much in evidence beneath the tangle of undergrowth. Donna was fascinated by the way in which each individual stone or rock had been shaped and fitted to form the smooth hard surface, all without the aid of cement.

'I know where it's going to,' she said over the campfire, 'but where does it come from?'

'That's a project for some other expedition to take up,' Blake responded. 'Maybe even from Cuzco itself, although tracing it through would be a devil of a job. Incanta lies due east of here, so it's possible the road ran right on through to the lowlands originally. We'll probably never know. It would take years to retrace the whole length of it, even allowing for the possibility that most of it still exists.'

'Remember the one at Incallacta?' put in Janine. 'It connects a series of forts and lookout points guarding Bolivian passes,' she added kindly for those less well informed. 'We were able to follow it for two days.' Her smile was for Blake only, slow and intimate. 'That was a very worthwhile six weeks, all told.'

'Wasn't it?' He was smiling back, voice deceptively indolent. 'But it's in the past, and irrelevant to our present interests, wouldn't you say?'

Donna held her breath as the woman's face darkened visibly. There were ways of putting someone down, and that had been deliberately cruel. If he could be so totally ruthless where Janine was concerned what kind of chance was he going to give her? He would use her the way he thought she deserved to be used and then discard her with just the same lack of regard.

To do her credit, Janine made a swift recovery from discomfiture, but from the glance she turned fleetingly in Donna's direction it was apparent at whose door she was laying the blame for her relegation. It would be easier to accept, Donna thought, if she knew the truth, yet there was no way she could bring herself to make that gesture. It was enough that Edith knew.

The night came in chill, but sheltered as they were from the wind, sleeping bags were deemed sufficient. The Quechua themselves seemed unaffected by changes in temperature, more concerned for the welfare of their animals than they were for themselves. Donna chose her own spot as far away as possible from Janine. Tomorrow at this time they would be at Incanta and organised into a proper camp. The three women were destined to share a tent, that much she knew. It was some comfort to know that Edith Remington would be there as a buffer.

Inevitably her thoughts turned to Blake. With weeks in his company still to be endured it was doubtful that she was going to emerge unscathed. Blake didn't care what others might think. If he wanted her he would take her. She could appeal for help, of course, but what could she say? To deny her own desire would be a lie. Right now she longed to feel him close, to know the tingling, spine-trembling touch of his hands on her skin. She moved restlessly inside the padded warmth of the sleeping bag, remembering the times they had made love in the past. Blake had been so adept at arousal, his long, clever fingers sensitive to every minute reaction on her part. Not that he'd ever had to wait long for her to reach the point of optimum enjoyment. Sometimes he had only to look at her with that slow smile of his to have her in flames.

Stop it! she told herself desperately at that point. In another moment or two she was going to be getting up and going to him, and what would the others think of that!

It was a long night. Rising with the rest around six-thirty, Donna avoided Blake's eyes, certain that he would know immediately what she was feeling. One conclusion she had reached: she didn't want any divorce. Yet could Blake ever learn to love again? From what he had said the other day it seemed doubtful. She had wounded him too deeply.

They came down on to the banks of a narrow but fast-flowing river after an hour or so's walking, finding yet more traces of ancient roadway deeply overgrown. The valley was steep-sided and winding, the lower slopes laced with scrub and stunted trees no higher than a man's shoulders. When they finally came within sight of the city itself it was whole minutes before anyone realised due to the obscuring effect of Andean vegetation.

Incanta stood where the valley floor rose to form a large and level platform before opening and dropping towards the east, its crumbling stone walls backing on to living rock. Below it the river tumbled in a series of cascades and waterfalls towards the forested lower valley, with the trail they had been following vanishing from sight around a spur of rock. The setting was supreme, the only approaches defensible against an army. To view it from above, the plane carrying Graham and Janine must have flown within the valley walls themselves, Donna realised. A dangerous manoeuvre indeed!

A narrow stony path led from the river to the walls of the city, climbing terraces which might once have been cultivated fields in the distant past. It was not an easy climb in the rarefied atmosphere still to be found at more than eight thousand feet above sea level, and Donna was not the only member of the party highly relieved to pass between the two crenellated sections of

Harlequin Presents...

VIOLET WINSPEAR
time of the temptress

SALLY WENTWORTH
say hello to yesterday

GET 4 BOOKS FREE

CHARLOTTE LAMB
man's world

ANNE MATHER
born out of love

Say Hello to Yesterday
Holly Weston had done it all alone.

She had raised her small son and worked her way up to features writer for a major newspaper. Still the bitterness of the the past seven years lingered.

She had been very young when she married Nick Falconer—but old enough to lose her heart completely when he left. Despite her success in her new life, her old one haunted her.

But it was over and done with—until an assignment in Greece brought her face to face with Nick, and all she was trying to forget....

Time of the Temptres:
The game must be played his way!

Rebellion against a cushioned, controlled life had landed Eve Tarrant in Africa. Now only the tough mercenary Wade O'Marc stood between her and possible death in the wild, revolution-tor jungle.

But the real danger was Wade himself—he had made Eve aware of herself as a woman.

"I saved your neck, so you feel you owe me something," Wade said. "But you don't owe me a thing, Eve. Get away from me." She knew she could make him lose his head if she tried. But tha wouldn't solve anything....

Your Romantic Adventure Starts Here.

Born Out of Love
It had to be coincidence!

Charlotte stared at the man through a mist of confusion. It was Logan. An older Logan, of course, but unmistakably the man who had ravaged her emotions and then abandoned her all those years ago.

She ought to feel angry. She ought to feel resentful and cheated. Instead, she was apprehensive—terrified at the complications he could create.

"We are not through, Charlotte," he told her flatly. "I sometimes think we haven't even begun."

Man's World
Kate was finished with love for good.

Kate's new boss, features editor Eliot Holman, might have deva tating charms—but Kate couldn care less, even if it was obvious that he was interested in her.

Everyone, including Eliot, thoug Kate was grieving over the loss her husband, Toby. She kept it a carefully guarded secret just ho cruelly Toby had treated her an how terrified she was of trusting men again.

But Eliot refused to leave her alone, which only served to infu ate her. He was no different fro any other man... or was he?

These FOUR free Harlequin Presents novels allow you to enter the world of romance, love and desire. As a member of the Harlequin Home Subscription Plan, you can continue to experience all the moods of love. You'll be inspired by moments so real... so moving... you won't want them to end. So start your own Harlequin Presents adventure by returning the reply card below. <u>DO IT TODAY!</u>

BUSINESS REPLY CARD

First Class   Permit No. 70   Tempe, AZ

POSTAGE WILL BE PAID BY ADDRESSEE

**Harlequin Reader Service
2504 W. Southern Avenue,
Tempe, Arizona 85282**

NO POSTAGE
NECESSARY
IF MAILED
IN THE
UNITED STATES

outer wall left standing. At close quarters it was easier to pick out the shapes of buildings hidden from below: first a group of small, single-room houses Blake said would have been occupied by workers, then on a series of shallow terraces, the remains of twenty-five or thirty larger dwellings with stone floors.

Further in lay sections of walling representing a building larger by far than any other on the site, some standing portions retaining shallow niches cut into their inner surface. To the right of this, and lifted on a platform reached via worn steps, stood a solid block of stone some six feet in length which had deep grooves cut into all four corners.

'Sacrificial,' Blake pronounced to those in the vicinity. 'The grooves would be used to secure the victim's limbs in position.'

'Human victims?' asked Donna, shuddering at the imagery.

'Not necessarily. Animals were often used too.' He glanced round at her with sardonically lifted brow. 'Don't get fainthearted. We're probably going to make some grisly finds once we start digging around.'

'I've seen skeletons before,' she responded without heat. 'We drained a *cenote* on the previous dig. If I had to choose I think I'd take drowning in preference to having my heart cut out!'

There was no one else close enough to hear his softly mocking reply. 'They only did that to virgins. I can vouch for your lack of qualifications in that particular department.'

'You should,' she said, refusing to let him get to her. 'You took it.'

'But only after I put a ring on your finger.' His glance had hardened. 'I notice you don't wear it.'

'I haven't worn it since we separated,' Donna confessed. 'It seemed . . . I didn't feel entitled.'

The grey eyes held an odd light in their depths. 'You're still married, even if it is only on paper. Why don't you tell the truth? You stopped wearing it because it limited your activities.'

Some perverse instinct shaped her reply. 'Your activities were hardly limited, were they? By your own admittance you had an affair with Janine Meade. Are you saying I should have considered myself still bound by promises you were more than willing to forget?'

'How many?' he demanded, ignoring the question. 'How many men have you known in the last two years?'

'If I told you you wouldn't believe me,' she said with irony. 'Forget it, Blake. We neither of us have any right to complain.'

'You'll tell me.' There was a threat in the bare statement. 'One day.' He turned and dropped down the stone steps from the altar.

The Quechua had set up camp down by the river, pitching the tents in a rough circle about the cooking area. There were five in all: four for human occupation and one for storage. The Indians themselves seemed content to bed down close by the corral they had made for their animals, with their own fire and cooking arrangements.

Looking up at the crumbling city as the last rays of the sun vanished behind the mountains, Donna tried to imagine the scene as it would have been some four hundred years ago, to see the buildings rearing in their proud entirety, to hear the sound of voices carried down on the breeze. Incanta had been a fortress city guarding the way from the east. As in all Inca cities, it had followed a religious way of life, hence the temple and altar stone. Tomorrow, when the sun rose again, it would fall directly on that place of sacrifice, once more finding it empty. Was it simply imagination which conjured up the faint sense of foreboding?

There was little time during the following days to think about anything beyond the job itself. Climbing the pathway to the city each morning took the better part of twenty minutes, although the strain began to lessen as the metabolism adjusted. Food for the day was taken with them and eaten cold, no one fancying the extra journey down to the cooking range. Fires on site were strictly forbidden by Blake owing to the dryness of the undergrowth. None of the party indulged in cigarettes; at this altitude it was oxygen, not nicotine, the lungs craved.

The Quechua proved invaluable when it came down to the rough work, clearing away the tangled growth to reveal more of the ruins, yet seeming to understand the need for care in their efforts. There were artefacts to be found, some still in usable condition, the pottery beautifully made and painted in reds and yellows. In the area of the temple itself were discovered several small statuettes in pure gold which caused a great deal of excitement. Once Donna had finished drawing and recording the dimensions of such items they were taken into the charge of Juan Prieto in the name of the Peruvian government, to be allowed out of the country only under licence for display purposes at some future date.

It was towards the end of the first week that they uncovered the burial chamber, and here Edith and Theo came into their own, spending patient hours examining the amazingly well preserved skeletons of a dozen or more bodies laid to rest so many centuries before. From the size of the chamber and its position, it was decided that this could very well be the burial place of the city's more important inhabitants—a kind of nobleman's tomb. Several of the skulls had a peculiar tapered shape which Edith declared was caused by the binding of the head from childhood to produce a distinguishing feature in the ruling class.

'They even had surgeons capable of brain surgery in those days,' she said one evening over supper. 'We've found more than one skull showing evidence of trepanning. I've seen an Inca surgeon's knife cut through bone with my own eyes. All it needed was sharpening. They were experts in metalwork.' She paused, looking across the circle of camp stools around the fire to where Donna sat. 'I'll want a detailed study of a skull showing a probable pre-frontal leucotomy. Can you handle it?'

'I'll give it my best,' Donna agreed, reserving doubt for a time when it might prove to be merited. 'The file's getting pretty thick already.'

'How's the site plan coming along?' asked Blake, taking time off from his discussion with Juan to join the conversation. 'It's important to keep it up to date as we work through.'

'I know.' Donna did her best to keep her tone neutral. 'You can examine it any time you want to.'

'No time like the present,' he said.

She came to her feet. 'I'll go and get it.'

'Don't bother.' His manner was easy. 'I may as well come with you to the tent.'

Walking across the rough grass at his side, Donna could feel Janine's eyes on her back. Over the past days few words had been exchanged between them, perhaps because of the restraining influence Edith's presence exerted. So far as Blake was concerned, she appeared to harbour no resentment. Certainly they worked together in perfect harmony. Yet what other choice did she have? They were all of them stuck here together for better or worse.

The tent shared with the other two women was neat and tidy, the three blow-up mattresses arranged T-shape, with personal possessions stored in plastic bags behind each one. Donna went down on her knees to secure her sketching satchel, taking out the larger of the two pads and twisting to get back to her feet again.

'Stay down there,' said Blake, and joined her on the mattress, sitting with one knee lifted to take an elbow as he reached for the pad in her hand. 'Let's see what you've got.'

'The first is the site plan in its entirety,' she explained. 'Then I'm taking it section by section as we excavate. Here's the temple, and here . . .' she reached out to turn a page, drawing in a sharp little breath as the side of her breast touched his arm '. . . here's the tomb, although it isn't quite finished yet. We really need photographs too, you know. Did you hear anything from Cuzco?'

'We'll have a photographer by this time day after tomorrow,' he said, 'but it won't be Graham. He's gone back to England.' He turned his head to look at her when she made no immediate reply, studying her face with narrowed eyes. 'You don't seem surprised.'

'I'm not,' she admitted. 'He told me he wouldn't be coming back.'

'Did he?' Blake sounded faintly disconcerted. 'That must have been a shock. Why didn't you go with him?'

'Because I had a job to do,' she defended. 'Anyway . . .' She broke off, realising where explanations could lead her. 'I had a job to do,' she repeated.

'You already said that.' His tone was quiet but edged with something infinitely disquieting. 'Did you think I'd forgotten what I said back in Cuzco?'

Donna shrugged, trying to retain control of the situation. 'It's irrelevant under the circumstances, isn't it?'

'Is it?' He let the sketch pad slide to the ground as he

took hold of her, finding her mouth in a kiss that rocked her senses, forcing response from her. The hand seeking her breast was fierce in its touch, yet the pain it inflicted only served to inflame her more. She moved blindly into him, giving way to the need to be close as once they had been close, feeling the hardness of his body driving the breath from her, the firm muscularity beneath her hands.

A burst of laughter from the group outside broke the spell, jerking her back to reality. From somewhere she found the strength to thrust herself away from him, her breath coming in shuddering little gasps. 'No, Blake!'

For a moment he seemed on the verge of dragging her back into his arms, then he made a visible effort to control himself. 'You're right,' he said. 'This isn't the place.' His face looked strained in the yellow light from the hanging lamp. 'Maybe we should let the whole matter rest till we get back to civilisation when we can see it in perspective. Taking you isn't going to solve anything.'

Donna sat without moving as he pushed himself to his feet. There was nothing left to say. Only when Blake had left the tent did she put out an unsteady hand to pick up the fallen sketch pad and put it carefully back in the satchel. If Blake had meant what he had said he would not be touching her again in any intimate sense. It was better that way, she knew, yet knowing it didn't help. How was she going to stand another seven weeks of wanting him the way she wanted him right now? The thought alone was almost more than she could bear.

The helicopter arrived on schedule two days later, bringing the promised photographer, who had a lot of catching up to do. He was in his early forties and of Spanish extraction. Meeting him for the first time, Donna registered the look which sprang in the dark eyes and felt her heart sink. Not more complications!

Suspicion was confirmed when he began making a point of staying close to her whenever opportunity offered itself. Where looks were concerned, he was a very attractive man, but he held no personal appeal for her. She wished he would simply get on with his job and leave her to get on with hers.

Blake himself seemed not to notice the newcomer's overtures, or if he did he was ignoring them. He was totally involved in the dig, his every spare moment spent delving deeper into the past of this long-dead city. After that time in the tent he had spoken to Donna only when necessary, any emotion he might still be feeling firmly under control. Interesting as she found her own work, she could not conjure up the same degree of detachment.

Other matters aside, there was something about Incanta that triggered her nerves, sounding an odd little warning bell at the back of her mind. Sometimes at night she would get up and go outside to reassure herself that everything was as it should be, because in her dreams she had felt the whole landscape trembling.

'Minor earth movements,' said Edith when she mentioned the matter. 'I felt one myself the other night. Nothing to worry about. They occur all the time in this part of the world.'

Donna was only partially reassured, the signal still strong inside her head. She had once read a book supporting the theory that old stone could record moments of great emotional impact and store them in much the same way as a modern-day tape recorder, awaiting certain stimuli to start playing them back. If there was anything in that theory then perhaps the stones of Incanta were reacting to something in her, sending out waves to disquiet her mind. If so then the danger she sensed was in the past and of no account. If not . . . Deliberately she let the thought lie. She was no clairvoyant.

Gradually as the days passed the need grew in her to escape the valley, yet she knew the others would never be persuaded by vague fears without substance to back them up. She was being an imaginative fool, she told herself on more than one occasion, yet she could not seem to shake the feeling that something was going to happen.

Her notion one afternoon to try following the river downstream some way stemmed as much from a desire to escape the attentions of Ramon Deta as the need to spend a little time on her own in order to think. In another week, Michael and Philip would be air-lifted out. What she had to decide was, did she want to go with them? A week ago the answer would have been no, but even the work had lost a great deal of its interest for her. She blamed Blake for that. How could she be expected to concentrate on producing a perfect drawing of a shard when all the time she was thinking of him? At night she ached to be with him, knowing full well she never would be again. Once they got back to civilisation he would set the wheels in motion for the divorce she had asked for. In the long run it had to be best for them both. The feeling they had left for each other was scarcely enough to sustain a marriage.

She had reached the point at which the trail curved out of sight behind a spur of rock before beginning its downward trend. Glancing back towards camp, she refused to feel guilty over her desertion. Sunday was supposedly their one day of rest, yet so far few had paid any attention to the rule. Janine had been the only one to notice her leaving. No doubt she would lose little time in pointing out her absence to Blake. Not that it mattered; he was hardly likely to come after her. Donna could almost hope that he would—at least she might have the chance to get him out of her system for good and all.

The view out over the lower valley was tremendous, the trail wide enough to take two men abreast on mule-back. The river was always within hearing if not in sight, its volume increased by the lofting waterfall which cut down past the citadel itself to join it. Water had played an important part in the religion of the Incas. Only by total immersion could the soul be purified. A strange race, mused Donna, where piety and cruelty had walked hand in hand; the skeletons of many young females found beneath the temple told their own story.

The trail split after some ten minutes or so of winding progress, one branch continuing in its downward trend, the other cutting back into a cleft in the hillside. Donna took the second path for the simple reason that it would be less of a strain to retrace her steps, following it through into another small valley with several exits to choose from. After so much time spent at altitude she felt little discomfort any more, providing she took things reasonably easy. Walking was pleasant with the sun still warm and the tough grasses springing beneath her feet. Unlike the lower valley for which she had originally been making, the vegetation here was sparse, lacking soil for deeper roots and taller growth. Once again the trail split in two, leading heaven only knew where and for what purpose. Intrigued, Donna chose the left-hand branch again, wondering if any other foot but hers had trodden this path since the Incas themselves had used it. It gave her an odd, almost eerie feeling to think that centuries might have passed since any human had looked on this landscape from ground level.

When she eventually came upon the neatly grouped pile of stones she knew at once why the path was there. This was a *wak'a* or shrine—a sacred place honoured by the ordinary people of the time. The sacrifices made here would almost certainly have been non-human, the offerings intended to placate the gods into sending good crops or allowing the sick to recover their health. Water would not be far away, although she could hear none running.

If she followed the same trail onwards she would probably find herself coming back to Incanta by a different route—very possibly a shorter one. That might not be a bad idea, she thought, taking a look at the sun which was already well down towards the western rim. This near the Equator there was little if any twilight. Once the sun set it would be pitch dark within a short time.

Looking down at yet another totally unfamiliar valley some forty minutes later, she was forced to concede that the idea had not after all been a good one. The only way left to her was to retrace her steps. The sun was in her eyes right now, and within half an hour of setting. If she turned her back on it and kept heading in the same direction she should be able to stay on the trail even after dark.

She was fooling herself and she knew it. There had been other trails criss-crossing the one she had followed, their purpose undefined. Already the air was cooling, making it necessary to don the sweater she had hitherto carried. If she had to spend the night out here it was going to be an uncomfortable one, Donna acknowledged, trying not to let the thought scare her out of her wits. She had been an idiot leaving the camp in the first place. This was no country for a Sunday afternoon stroll. So far they had seen little if any wildlife, but that wasn't to say it didn't exist. The puma was reputed to inhabit these levels. By all accounts it was a shy animal, not often seen by man, yet hunger could conquer a whole lot of inhibitions. She didn't even have a match to light a protecting fire, although fuel lay all about her in the shape of scrubby bush and trees.

Cloud rolling in from the south obscured the sky, bringing full darkness within bare moments of sunset. The rain shower didn't last long, but it was heavy enough to soak her to the skin. Shivering, she began to wonder if she would even make it through the night. At eight thousand feet it wasn't going to freeze, but temperatures could drop as low as six or seven degrees centigrade at this time of year. Even allowing for her youth and excellent state of health, hours of exposure in wet clothing could do her nothing but harm.

She had been stumbling along for what seemed an age when she first heard the cry. It seemed to come from a great distance, eerie in the dark landscape. Donna stopped moving and strained her ears to listen, trying to shut out the other sounds of the night. Fear suggested a mountain cat on the hunt, even while common sense told her that no animal would vocalise its presence on such an errand.

There it was again, no closer yet definitely no animal either. Cupping her hands to her mouth, she called 'Here!' as loudly as she could manage, repeating the word once more before pausing to listen again. For a heart-stopping moment or two there was no answer. When it did come she felt faint from sheer relief. That was a human voice, and it was calling her by name. A male voice for certain, if not immediately identifiable. She didn't care who it was providing he found her.

She saw the beam of the torchlight before she heard the sound of approach. By that time she was too hoarse from shouting to raise more than a whisper of greeting.

'Thank heaven!'

She knew it was Blake by his very lack of response. The tautness of his anger reached her before he did. Blinking in the beam of light thrown up into her face, she tried to control the chattering of her teeth, too well aware of the sorry picture she must present.

'I'd say the first priority is warmth,' he stated flatly, not attempting to touch her. 'There's a cave of sorts in the rocks some way back. If you hold on to my backpack I'll lead the way. You're capable of walking about half a mile?'

Right then Donna felt incapable of anything very much. She wanted simply to be warm and dry again. She nodded numbly, not trusting her voice.

Those few hundred yards were the longest she had ever covered in her life, her feet stumbling over every tussock of grass, every ridge of bare rock. Long before they reached the outcrop and found the shallow cleft she was exhausted and close to collapse. Only the knowledge of Blake's scorn kept her from giving way altogether.

He left her sitting on the hard but mercifully dry ground while he went to forage for wood for a fire. Within minutes of his return he had a blaze going at the entrance, positioned so that the smoke drifted out to the side rather than over the two of them. There was little enough room to move, but the spreading warmth was bliss. Donna held out grateful hands to the flames.

'Get those wet clothes off,' ordered Blake roughly, opening up the pack he had brought with him. 'I packed a couple of the heat sheets just in case, although I didn't bargain for the rain.'

'I don't suppose it's much use my saying I'm sorry for acting so stupidly,' said Donna on a husky note. 'Did you come out alone?'

'The men split to cover all possible directions once it was realised you were missing. It was sheer luck that I happened to be the one to follow this route. I found your footprints back at the *wak'a* just before sunset, so at least I knew I was on the right track.' He paused, drawing in a long slow breath as if for control. '*Why*, Donna? Why just walk out without a word to anybody? Have you lost your senses completely!'

'Janine saw me go,' she defended. 'Didn't she tell you?'

'You must be mistaken.' His tone left no room for argument. 'I told you to get out of those wet things. I'm going to do the same. The sheets are big enough to wrap round once they're unfolded. They feel thin, but the thermoplastic will keep out the cold. If we keep the fire going good and strong and drape things over the rocks there they may be dry enough by morning. We don't have any other choice.'

'We're staying here all night?' Donna recognised the foolishness of the question the moment she finished asking it, but it was too late to retract. She bit her lip when Blake didn't even bother to reply. Whatever he was thinking she deserved.

He went to collect more fuel while she got out of her clothes, returning to dump an armload as she drew the sheet about her nearly nude body. Face totally devoid of expression, he stripped off his own clothing and wrapped himself in the other sheet, sitting close though not quite touching, knees bent up to his chin.

'Hungry?' he asked after a painful pause. 'I only have chocolate but sugar is sustaining. There's a thermos of coffee too, only I think we should save that for later when it's likely to be colder.'

'You thought of everything,' Donna commented, intending no sarcasm. 'Do you think the others will have got back to camp before dark?'

'If they've any sense.'

'You didn't turn back.'

'I knew I wasn't on a wild goose chase.' The smile held irony. 'I was wild enough myself a while back. If I'd got my hands on you while it was still light I'd have half strangled you!'

Her voice sounded faint and faraway. 'Only while it was light?'

'Darkness brings a new element to any search. Concern becomes the major emotion. By the time I found you I was too relieved to contemplate violence.'

'That's not how it felt.'

Blake turned his head to look at her in the flickering firelight, his features sharply etched. 'That wasn't anger you felt. It isn't anger I'm feeling now. I'd intended leaving you strictly alone for the rest of the time we were here, but I didn't count on this. It's going to be a long night, Donna. Don't make it even longer by fighting me through it.'

She could find no words to express her emotions as he reached for her. His lips felt cold against hers, but not for long. He took the sheet from about her shoulders and spread it on the ground, pressing her down on to it and drawing the other one over the two of them before starting to kiss her again, his mouth as hungry and urgent as the hands which roved her body.

There was little left to remove for either of them. Held close against his male hardness, Donna gave free rein to the passion so long held in check, moaning her need as she dug her nails into the broad back; offering herself to him with an eagerness that inflamed him to swift and devastating conclusion.

'That was for me,' he murmured into her hair when breath and sense returned. 'Now we'll start again, this time with finesse.'

He began with a kiss, just the merest brushing of lips against lips, developing by slow degrees until her mouth was mobilised to feverish demand, her whole mind centred on this one moving, searching contact. Only when he sensed her total abandonment did he move onwards down the line of her throat to her breasts, circling each hardened, tingling nipple with the tip of his tongue while she writhed under him, drawing wordless little whimpers of sound from deep down in her throat.

In the timeless moments following the world contracted to this one small dark cave, mind and body governed by the intimate use of lip and tongue, by the feel of strong and ruthless hands, by the sheer agony of wanting. And then at last, at long, long last, the coming together, like two halves of one whole, the giving and taking until the earth itself moved and shattered into a trillion tiny pieces.

CHAPTER SEVEN

DONNA was first to awaken when light began to filter into the cave. Replenished during the night, the fire still smouldered, needing only a fresh supply of fuel to liven it into flame. Wrapped in Blake's arms she felt warm as toast—inside as well as out, she thought mistily, studying the familiar features so close to her own. Last night had been a whole new experience, one she never wanted to forget; one she never could forget. To say she had fallen in love all over again would be a lie, inasmuch as she had never really loved before. What she had felt for Blake two years ago paled into insignificance before this aching, blinding emotion. Whatever happened now she couldn't give him up; she *wouldn't* give him up! They were husband and wife. She wanted the whole wide world to know that fact.

Gently she brought up a hand and touched the firm lips, remembering the pleasure they had afforded her in the night. Feeling him stir, she went very still, waiting for the moment when he would open his eyes and see her. Her hair was a tangled mess, but she didn't care. The experience they had shared went deeper than surface appearances.

He came awake slowly, looking at her with blankness for several seconds before memory flashed into being. Just for an instant she saw warmth in the grey depths, even the beginnings of tenderness, then the colour changed, hardening to a steel-like opacity she could no longer read.

'We'd better see if our clothes are dry,' he said, and rolled away from her to sit up and reach out for the nearest garments. 'The shirts seem okay,' he announced a moment or two later. 'We'll just have to put up with damp legs. Your sweater is still wet. You can have my anorak till the sun gets up.'

Donna hadn't moved, too frozen in mind to feel the chill on her body. What she had expected from him she wasn't even sure any more. Only certainly it had not been this. He was acting as if nothing at all had happened between them—as if last night had just been a dream on her part. For a wild moment she actually wondered if it had been, but the physical reminders were real enough. Blake had made love to her not just once but again and again, until they had both been satiated. Her body stirred at the very memory, her arms folding across her breasts as if in belated protection.

'Don't treat me this way,' she whispered painfully. 'Don't pretend it all meant nothing to you.'

He looked at her then, the hardness unrelenting. 'Last night was one thing, today is something else,' he said. 'You were the one who asked for a divorce, remember? Well, you can have it. I shan't oppose it. I've had everything I wanted from you, Donna—every last ounce of payment. I don't pretend it meant nothing to me. Few women can give a man that degree of pure satisfaction. It might have been enough once. These days . . .' He stopped and shook his head, his mouth taking on a slant. 'That's beside the point. Just get dressed.'

Donna sat up, letting the sheet fall away from her shoulders without even noticing. 'Blake, I love you,' she said desperately. 'Not like before. I'm older now.'

'And wiser?' The slant increased. 'What you feel for me is pure and simple lust, sweetheart. That's all it ever was. You don't love me. You don't even know me. I just happen to be one man who can apparently satisfy you more than any other you've met, but that doesn't make me the only one capable. Keep on looking. You might strike lucky. So might he—for a limited period!'

'You bastard!' Her face was white.

'That's right.' He was totally unmoved. 'And who made me one?' He tossed her shirt and trousers to her, thrusting aside the sheet to start pulling on his own things. 'We never got round to having that coffee. It should still be lukewarm. I want to be back in camp before they start organising another search party. It will be light enough to move out in twenty minutes or so.'

Donna forced her limbs into movement, her fingers nerveless as they dealt with buttons and zips. The sheer calculation of it all hurt the most. Blake had stripped her of every last vestige of pride. With nothing to lose, she found it in herself to make one last plea.

'Did no one ever have a second chance with you, Blake?'

'It would depend,' he said without turning, 'on how they fouled up the first one. I don't think you have it in you to feel anything very deep for any man. At any rate, I'm not willing to risk getting involved again. You've heard the saying, once bitten, twice shy?'

'How original!' she mocked bitterly.

'But apt.' He refused to rise to the taunt. 'If it's any consolation, I still want you. In fact, I could take you again right now.' His tone had roughened. 'That's a price I'll have to go on paying. Do you want some coffee?'

She would have liked to tell him what to do with his coffee, but where was the point? Abuse was unlikely to stir him to anything outside anger. She took the thermos cup he offered, putting her lips to the barely warm liquid with a feeling that she was never going to be rid of the ice forming deep down inside her.

'At least I still have my job,' she said, fighting to sound philosophical about it. 'I do, don't I?'

'If you want it.' There was no give in him. 'I don't have any faults to find with your work.'

They moved out in silence some fifteen minutes later when the light was good enough to see rock and root. The sun was just showing above the horizon by the time they reached the *wak'a*. It was here that they met up with Juan Prieto and Michael, who had set out to follow in Blake's footsteps.

The return to camp and subsequent explanations and recriminations took up half the morning. Janine was the only one who stayed aloof. Later, Donna saw Blake having a word with her. Perhaps the relationship was on again now that he had rid his mind of other intruding factors, she reflected painfully. It was no use telling herself she didn't care, because she did. The feeling she had for Blake stemmed from a place inviolate to persuasion. Life was going to be hard no matter how he conducted himself these coming weeks. If she had any sense she would get out when the first opportunity arose. They could find another artist the same way they had found another photographer.

Not for the first time she thought about Graham with guilt, wondering what he was doing right now. Perhaps after all they belonged together. At least with Graham she would never know this degree of hurt.

Yes, but what about him? she was bound to ask herself. Didn't he deserve something better than to be used as a bolthole? Left alone, he might one day find a love wholly and freely given. He certainly should have the chance. When she returned to England she had to make her own life, without help from anyone. Running away from this job would not further her career.

Janine waited for a moment that evening when she and Donna were alone in their shared tent before letting go with what was on her mind.

'Just as a matter of interest,' she said, 'it might pay

you to know Blake is already married, so any ideas you might have about him you can forget. It's been a long time since spending a night with a man committed him to anything.' She looked across to where Donna sat sorting through a pile of sketches, her brows lifting. 'You don't seem surprised.'

'As a matter of fact, I'm not.' Donna was hard put to keep irony at bay. 'I've known about his marriage all along. He's estranged from his wife, though, isn't he?'

'Yes, only that won't help you any either. If he marries again it won't be to a no-account like you.'

This time Donna forced herself to look up. 'What makes you so sure I'd want to marry him in the first place?'

'Because you're the type to use your body with purpose.' The tone was scathing. 'And don't try making out that nothing happened between the two of you last night, because I'm not going to believe it. I'm old enough to recognise a certain look about those who've indulged recently. I don't blame Blake. After all, when a girl makes it as obvious as you've made it that she's his for the asking, few men are going to turn her down!'

The initial accusation had rankled because it might once have been true. Not that Donna had any intention of letting the other woman know it. 'That's not giving him much credit for taste or discrimination, is it?' she said. 'A man who'd have *any*body!'

Janine lifted a lip. 'I'm not so insecure that I need to run down another female's looks. Blake has a particular weakness for blondes.'

'I'm sure he has.' Donna could feel the pain building up, urging her to lash out at her tormentor with a few well-placed, irrefutable facts. She held on to her self-control by the skin of her teeth. 'If it's any reassurance to you, I'm only too well aware that Blake Mitchell is his own man. He'll do exactly as *he* wants to do, and neither you nor I will influence him!'

'You, maybe not.' There was no putting Janine down. 'Just so long as we have things quite clear.' She turned as Edith Remington pushed aside the tent flap, treating the older woman to a brief nod. 'I'll see you later. There's too much of a crowd in here.'

'Depends on the three,' drawled Edith with irony as the archaeologist left the tent. She gave Donna a thoughtful look. 'What's been going off?'

'Nothing,' Donna denied. She held the unwavering gaze for a moment, then sighed. 'Nothing important, anyway. She came to ask me if I knew Blake was already married.'

Edith's laugh was short. 'You didn't tell her?'

'No.'

'Why not?'

'Because it won't be true for all that much longer.' Donna refused to let emotion take over. 'Blake wants a divorce as much as I do.'

'I can't speak for him,' said Edith after a moment, 'but I don't think it's what you want. I've seen you change towards him these last days. I've seen you watching him when you thought no one was watching you. I'm not asking you to tell me what went wrong between you two in the first place—that's between you and Blake—only it's surely worth trying to salvage a marriage before giving up completely.'

'There's no chance of that.' Donna said it with all the flat conviction she could muster. 'Please believe me, Edith, there's nothing left to salvage.'

'You have to know best.' It was obvious that the older woman wanted to say more, but she held it back. 'Carlos has just made fresh coffee. Why don't you come and have some? If it's any incentive, Blake is looking over today's findings with Theo and Juan in their tent.'

'Thanks.' Donna was grateful for the concern. 'I think I will.'

It was full moon that night. Waking around one-thirty, Donna knew a sudden and full return of the trepidations that had bothered her before. Stifled by the confines of the tent, she reached silently for her outdoor clothing and crept through the flap, shivering a little as the chill hit her. The silence seemed almost tangible, the moon highlighting a landscape devoid of movement from even the merest breath of wind. From here the citadel itself was invisible, yet it exercised an irresistible pull.

Without pausing to consider her actions rationally, Donna clad herself in pants and anorak over her pyjamas and tugged on socks and boots, then got to her feet to start the climb to the main entrance. There was no sense of loneliness, just of being alone. Pure instinct guided her feet up the steep track, the sound of her breathing unnaturally loud on the chill air. Below she could see the camp, the embers of the fire still glowing on the stone platform at its hub. Nothing stirred down there. They might all be dead for all she knew.

By moonlight the city should have been eerie, but somehow it was far from that. The feeling of dread came from inside, not out. Standing in the middle of the open space that had once been the central plaza, Donna listened to the silence, wondering at its totality. It was as if the earth itself was holding its breath. The sound of a human voice only partially shattered the illusion.

'If you followed me up here to try for a repeat of last night's performance, you're going to be out of luck,' came the harsh statement. 'It's over, Donna.'

She swung abruptly to find Blake watching her from under the remaining semi-curve of the temple doorway, one booted foot resting on a piece of fallen masonry. He was dressed as she was herself in padded anorak and cord jeans.

'I couldn't sleep,' she said. 'I had no idea you were up here.' Her tone hardened to match his own. 'You can believe that or not, just as you like.'

He studied her, his face austere. Even as he opened his mouth to speak again the air seemed to shimmer between them, distorting his features. Donna felt the rumble before she heard it, and fell to her knees as the ground under her lost its stability and began to shudder and shake to the accompaniment of a sickening, roaring, thundering sound that was everywhere about her. A fissure opened up suddenly only bare feet from where she clutched the heaving earth, running the full width of the plaza towards the temple. She knew she was screaming yet could hear no sound issuing from her lips above the chaos of falling masonry and splitting rock. Both the temple doorway and Blake himself had vanished behind a cloud of dust and debris. She was entirely alone in a world gone mad.

When it finally ended the sudden silence was shattering. Donna stayed crouched down where she was for several long seconds while the dust settled about her, not really believing it was over. At the back of her mind a memory was emerging—something about aftershocks. She had to get away from this place while the going was good—to where she wasn't sure.

Blake! With sense and sanity returning she raised her head to take a look around. The terrain had altered visibly, many of the old walls no longer standing. Where the temple entrance had been lay a heap of rubble. All she could see of Blake was one outstretched arm, the fist clenched and unmoving.

She had to step across the foot-wide crack in the ground to reach him, shuddering at the blackness within. There was no knowing how deep it went. For all she knew it might go clear to the base of the platform on which the city was built. Blake lay in the midst of the debris from the arch. There were several smaller stones lying across his back and legs, and one stained black with his blood close by his head. Donna put out her hand to take his wrist between finger and thumb, forcing herself to stay rational. He was alive, but the pulse was thin and fluttery. She set about clearing the rubble away from his body, trying to ascertain whether any limbs were broken. So far as she could tell from a cursory examination in these conditions they were intact. Not that the knowledge was all that comforting. Broken bones would heal; head wounds were so much more dangerous. He needed the kind of help she couldn't provide, and he needed it fast.

Working with a speed and efficiency born of sheer desperation, she stripped off her anorak and made a pillow of it, lifting the dark head with tender caution. The wound was above and to the front of the right temple, a frighteningly large and sticky mess she made no attempt to touch. Her pyjama jacket was thin, but she was unaware of any chill. Somehow she had to get down to the camp and organise a stretcher party. Always providing the others had come through the earthquake in one piece themselves. Things might have been even worse down there with rock crashing from above. She dreaded to imagine what she might find.

It took her more than half an hour to make the journey owing to the fact that the track had all but vanished in places, leaving bare, broken rock in its place. Before she reached the bottom her hands were scraped raw from her many falls, her pyjama top ripped across the back.

She found the camp in considerable chaos, the tents down, the area itself lifted into an unrecognisable series of ridges and dips. Someone had salvaged a couple of the Calor-gas lamps, lending the scene an unearthly yellow glow that enhanced the sense of disaster. Edith was the first to see Donna, dropping the box she held in her arms with a look of mingled relief and astonishment.

'Where were you, girl?' she demanded. 'We've been looking for you and Blake for the past half hour!'

'We were up in the city,' Donna gasped. 'Blake's still up there. He's badly injured—head wound. He needs help, Edith. We have to go to him!'

'Steady!' Theo was suddenly there with them, his arm comfortingly strong and supportive. 'We have some injuries down here too, though fortunately not too serious. I'll get Michael and Juan and Carlos. Between the four of us we should manage to get him down. Is he conscious?'

'Not when I left him.'

'Then we'll need to improvise a stretcher of sorts. We've already contacted Cuzco by radio. The quake didn't even reach there. By all accounts it wasn't a very bad one, but we appear to have been close to the epicentre.'

Edith found a thick sweater and insisted Donna should put it on. 'You need to sit down,' she said. 'You're still in shock.'

'I'm going back,' Donna stated, ignoring the trembling of her limbs. 'I know where he is.'

'You can explain to the men. They all know the city well enough to follow directions.' Edith was kind but firm. 'The last thing they're going to need is another casualty.'

Donna had to see the sense in the argument even while every instinct in her cried out to reject it. To wait here while others went to Blake's aid was going to be the most difficult thing she had ever done in her life. Not knowing whether he was alive or dead was the worst part. She daren't allow herself to dwell on a future in which Blake no longer even existed.

Dawn was breaking by the time the rescue party returned. They came slowly and with difficulty, supporting the stretcher improvised out of anoraks with tent poles pushed up the sleeves. Blake was alive but still deeply unconscious, his face deathly pale beneath the coating of blood and dust. A dressing had been applied to his wound, held in place by a bandage which hid most of his hair. Donna forcibly held herself back from over-emotionalism, aware that only Edith would understand the degree of her involvement. The helicopter would be here as soon as the light improved enough. Until then they could only wait.

Janine had been among those injured in the quake, her leg gashed below the knee by a falling rock. When the helicopter finally came in on its first mercy mission, she took it on herself to accompany Blake, sitting in the rear seat with his bandaged head cushioned on her lap.

Watching the machine lift into the air again, Donna felt as if she were being torn apart. By the time the rest of them reached Cuzco he could well be dead and gone. By rights she was the one who should be sitting there in support, not Janine, yet Blake himself would not have wanted her. It's over, he had said. How prophetic those words might yet be!

The after-shock when it came was mild enough to be virtually undetectable. With the last of the wounded despatched, Theo made the decision to strike camp and head back to civilisation with what they had for the present. Once in Cuzco he planned on reorganising a return trip with new equipment to replace that damaged in the quake. Despite the loss of much of the remaining citadel there was still a great deal of work to be done, he declared.

Donna stayed with the main party, because as one of the fit and well members left she could not bring herself to ask for special treatment. Blake's safe arrival in hospital was duly reported by radio, but further bulletins over the next few days of packing and travelling confirmed that there had been little change in his condition. Comas could last for years, Donna knew. The thought of that fine strong mind and body slowly wasting away was unbearable. It would be better, she told herself numbly, for him to die than to live as a cabbage.

They reached Cuzco on the evening of the fourth day after the earthquake, returning to the same house they had left less than three short weeks before. Met by the recuperating injured of the party, they were told that Blake had been transferred only that morning down to a private clinic in Lima where he would have the attention of one of the country's leading specialists. Janine had not accompanied him.

'I'm going back to Incanta,' she announced firmly over dinner. 'There's nothing any of us can do for Blake but hope for a recovery.' Briefly her eyes sought Donna's, revealing a certain surprising empathy. 'It's a dreadful thing to see a man like Blake Mitchell lying there like a corpse. I wouldn't wish the experience on my worst enemy.'

If you loved him you'd have stayed with him regardless, Donna thought, and wished she only had the chance. At the moment she had little idea what she was going to do next.

It took Edith to put matters into perspective later on when she came across her sitting in a corner of the salon gazing vacantly into space.

'Your heart isn't in going back to Incanta,' she said bluntly, 'so why bother? Passengers we can do without.'

Donna could not dispute the fact. For the present her interest in the past was dead. She lifted slim shoulders, meeting kindly eyes with rueful expression.

'You're saying I should just go on home and forget about it all?'

'No, I'm not saying that. You've a husband who needs you, even if he doesn't know it.' Edith shook her head to the rejection she could see taking shape. 'It doesn't matter what happened before. You're still married to him now. Why don't you go to him?'

Donna was silent for a long moment or two, searching the older woman's face with slowly dawning hope. 'You really think I should?'

'Isn't that what I just said? If you take the morning flight down with Michael and Philip you could be with him by lunchtime.' The smile was faint. 'Love is supposed to move mountains—bringing a man back to life should be child's play! The least you can do is give it a try.'

'Yes, I can, can't I.' Donna bent forward impulsively and kissed the lined cheek. 'Thank you. I needed someone to point me in the right direction. I'm going to pack.'

'Take care,' came the soft injunction as she got up from the sofa. 'We'll miss you.'

Janine made no such claim, though agreeing that Donna would be well advised not to return to Incanta.

'Your work is okay,' she admitted grudgingly, 'but you're nowhere near dedicated enough to last through an extensive dig without other interests. Now Blake is gone you might just as well go on home. Nervous exhaustion is an adequate reason for leaving a job halfway through. It shouldn't affect your chances of getting others.'

Donna responded with what sincerity she could muster, forced to acknowledge that in spite of everything the archaeologist had only acted the way any woman might act over a man she desired for herself. The fact that her emotion did not extend itself to any great depth could only be to the good so far as she,

Donna, was concerned. At least it left the way clear. The question of how she was going to cope if Blake regained consciousness and still rejected her, she preferred to leave unanswered. There would be time enough to consider alternatives if and when it happened.

Lima still sported the same band of coastal fog, the humidity enervating. Donna parted from her two companions at the airport, where they were to take an onward flight, passing through the barriers to find a cab to take her to the clinic. Finding somewhere to stay could come later. First she had to see Blake.

Once more she found herself heading for Miraflores, turning in eventually though the gates of yet another large and imposing residence set in extensive grounds. The fees for treatment in such a place must be astronomical, Donna realised. She wondered who was doing the paying. Blake had a private income from his father's estate in addition to his own earnings, she knew, but that still didn't make him wealthy enough to afford long-term residence at the Arguedas clinic.

A white-coated receptionist took down details in the spacious tiled entrance hall, asking Donna to wait in faultless English as she lifted a telephone receiver. Her Spanish was too rapid to follow. Donna could only wait the outcome with impatience and not a little dread. It had been almost a week since she had last seen Blake. Surely by now there had to be some development. If he was conscious he might of course refuse to see her at all, yet she somehow doubted if he would be that vindictive. Illness cut through many barriers.

A doctor arrived in answer to the call. He was a man in his fifties in whom Donna found a certain reassurance because he reminded her of Juan Prieto. He made no attempt to conceal surprise.

'We were not informed that Professor Mitchell was a married man,' he said. 'But now that you are here perhaps we shall see improvement.'

'He's still unconscious, then?' asked Donna unhappily.

'He responds to certain stimuli, from time to time. The next few days are the critical ones. If he is going to come out of it at all it should be then. He has not needed total life-support, which has to be a good sign, but we can only wait. Come, I will take you to him.'

Blake lay in a private room on the first floor, a still and silent figure with bandaged head and drained features, a drip running into the back of one hand. Only when Dr Vallego spoke could Donna perceive any movement, and that only the merest flicker of an eyelid.

'You try,' urged the doctor. 'Your voice has to be the one he is most likely to recognise. Take his hand, let him feel your warmth. There is every chance that the receptive areas are working normally, even though he remains outwardly comatose.'

Donna obeyed the instructions, sitting down in the chair already placed by the bedside to close her fingers about his lean brown hand. 'Blake,' she said softly. 'Blake, it's me, Donna. Wake up! You've slept long enough.' She paused, searching the sharply boned face on the pillow before looking across at the doctor with defeat in her eyes. 'Nothing.'

'You are wrong.' The doctor was holding the other wrist, fingers on the pulse. 'There is a response. It is only faint, true, but it proves that something is getting through. Try again, *señora*. Keep on trying. Only perseverance will reap any reward.'

He left her there to get on with it in the quiet, white-painted room during the whole of that long afternoon, a passage of time interrupted only once when coffee and sandwiches were brought to her. Of what she talked about during those hours she had afterwards little real idea. She said whatever came into her head, eyes always on the alert for any sign of life. Once or twice there seemed to be movement behind the closed eyelids, and at one point she was almost sure Blake's lips twitched, yet no miracle happened.

By six o'clock she could scarcely keep her own eyes open, and she still had to find somewhere to sleep that night. She rang the bell to bring a nurse to the room, wryly shaking her head to the unspoken question.

'Still the same. I'm afraid I'm going to have to leave for a while. I need to find a hotel close by.'

'A room has been prepared for you here at the clinic,' came the unexpected reply. 'Dr Vallego's orders. A meal will be brought to you when you are ready.' The nurse smiled and shook her head as Donna cast a hesitant glance back to the bed. 'He will not run away. Neither will he be left alone. Go now and rest.'

Dr Vallego came to see her in the charming bed-sitting room after she had eaten, taking a chair at her invitation.

'Today was merely a beginning,' he said. 'Tomorrow and the next day, and the day after that, you must try again—and keep on trying until you rouse him to life. There is no obvious physical reason why he should not make a full recovery. It all depends on the will. Is he a man of strong willpower, would you say?'

'Very.' That was one question she could answer without any shadow of doubt. She hesitated before asking a question of her own. 'Dr Vallego, could you give me some idea of what all this might be going to cost? My husband isn't a poor man, but neither is he a millionaire.'

'All has been taken care of,' he returned imperturbably. 'The Linden Foundation owns the clinic, and pays me well for my time. Naturally it is considered the Foundation's responsibility to see that Professor Mitchell receives the best of attention for injuries contracted during the course of his involvement.'

The relief was considerable. Not that it was by any means the main issue on her mind. 'What are the chances of complete recovery?' she asked carefully. 'I mean, if and when he does come round, is there likely to be any . . . impairment of any kind?'

The lift of his shoulders paid her the compliment of undisguised truth. 'Who can tell? The brain is still a largely unexplored region. We can hope.' He regarded her pale features with fatherly eyes as he rose to his feet again. 'You must sleep. I brought along a mild sedative to help you do so. Tomorrow may bring success, and you have to be fit to deal with it.'

Tomorrow did not bring success, nor the day after that. Donna spent almost every waking moment at Blake's bedside, letting her mind wander as she talked into his unresponsive ear, telling him things she had never told anyone in her life before. Apart from the times when it was necessary to change his drip, they remained undisturbed, two people alone together in a sterile room.

The breakthrough finally came on the third morning. Donna was talking about the early days of their marriage, smiling over their first real quarrel which had ended up, like most of the others, in bed. The sudden realisation that the grey eyes were open and turned towards her froze her in mid-sentence, her mouth about to frame the next letter.

'You look like a goldfish,' he murmured, so low that she could scarcely catch the words. 'And I feel like one! What happened?'

Donna jammed a finger down on the bell before answering, half laughing, half crying in shock and joy combined. 'You had an accident,' she said. 'But it's going to be all right now. Don't try to talk, Blake. Not until Dr Vallego has seen you.'

A frown drew his brows together. 'Vallego? Who's Vallego? Where am I, anyway?'

'Don't strain, please!' she begged. 'He'll be here in a moment. Oh, Blake, I've been so worried!'

The frown vanished, an unbelievable tenderness infiltrating his gaze. With difficulty he lifted his free hand to her face, obviously taken aback by his own weakness. 'Darling, you don't have to cry—I'm going to be fine. God, what a thing to happen on honeymoon! The last thing I remember is the wedding itself. How far did we get?'

CHAPTER EIGHT

DONNA was still sitting in stunned silence when Dr
Vallego came swiftly into the room. In the moments
following there was little opportunity to think about
anything beyond the awaited verdict as tests were made
on pupil reaction and oral clarity.

'There seems to be little more that I have to
do,' announced the Spanish medical man finally on
a note of satisfaction. 'You have made an excellent
recovery, *sênor*. You are both to be congratu-
lated.'

Blake was looking confused. 'Which hospital is this?'
he asked, eyeing the olive-skinned nurse hovering on
the edge of the scene.

Dr Vallego answered before Donna could put in a
word. 'No hospital, my friend. You are in the Arguedas
Clinic under the protection of the Linden Foundation.
It is the finest of its kind in the whole of Lima, that I
can assure you.'

'Lima?' The confusion increased. 'I don't understand.
What on earth . . .'

'Blake, it's all right.' Donna put her hand over his,
willing him to stay calm. 'I'll explain in a minute.' She
glanced across at Dr Vallego, biting her lip. 'Can I
speak to you for a moment?'

He took her out to the corridor, leaving the nurse to
minister to the man they left in total bewilderment
inside. 'There is something wrong, yes?' he declared.
'The memory is not functioning with total recall,
perhaps?'

'The memory is short of roughly thirty months,'

130

Donna told him, trying to retain some measure of calmness herself. 'He believes we were on our honeymoon when the accident happened. Our wedding day, to be exact.'

'I see.' The words held a wealth of comprehension. 'An unusual occurrence, but not without precedent. The memory appears to be located in the cereberal hemi-spheres, which is where in your husband's case the pressure had built. You could almost compare it to an electrical short-circuit. A part of the memory has in effect burnt out.'

'Can it repair itself?'

'That again is not predictable. It may, it may not. Perhaps you had best not place too much reliance on the former.'

Donna's mind was whirling as she tried to assimilate the factors involved. First and foremost, Blake believed them only just married—right at the beginning of their whole relationship. So far as he was concerned consummation had not even taken place. The memory of the way he had looked at her just now was one to treasure. Her pulses quickened as the full implications began to come home. He would have to be told, of course. There was no way of ignoring the intervening years. Yet did he have to know it all? If she kept her head and watched her tongue they could make a new start from this very moment. It would be living a lie, but with so much at stake surely an excusable one? Could she do it?

Blake was lying propped against the pillows when she returned to the room. He watched her approach with questioning, uncomprehending eyes.

'I can't think straight,' he said. 'Donna, what's happening? How did I get here? We *were* married this morning, weren't we? I didn't dream it?'

'You didn't dream it,' she said, taking the hand stretched towards her. 'Only it wasn't this morning.'

'No?' His eyes narrowed in concentration. 'Then when?'

'Two and a half years ago.' She saw the pupils dilate as shock coursed through him, and was thankful for Dr Vallego's presence. 'I'm sorry, darling. No matter which way I said it I couldn't make it sound any better. You have a head injury, and you've been unconscious for over a week. Somehow you've forgotten everything that's happened since the day we were married.'

'Two and a half years!' He repeated the words in tones of blank disbelief. 'It doesn't seem possible!'

'It is, however, true,' Dr Vallego picked up a copy of that day's newspaper which Donna had been skimming through earlier in an effort to take her mind off her worries for a moment or two. 'Look at the date. That must convince you.'

It did. Blake sank back into the pillows, the effort of adjustment visible in the tense lines of his face. 'You're going to have a lot of filling in to do,' he said at length. 'Supposing you start with here and now. What are we doing in Lima?'

'Shouldn't he rest first?' appealed Donna to the doctor, reluctant even now to take that irrevocable step.

'Dammit, I've had all the rest a man could need in the last week!' Blake's tone was rough, his jaw clenched 'Just tell me, Donna. All of it!'

Dr Vallego nodded. 'It would be best to get it out of the way. Ring if you need me.'

Meeting the waiting grey eyes, Donna swallowed dryly. The choice was hers, and it had to be made right now. She could either tell him the truth and see disillusionment take shape, or she could open a whole new past for them both, filling in detail to her own advantage. The memory of these last few weeks was all the incentive she really needed. Slowly and carefully she began to speak:

'We were on a dig in the Sierras—a place called Incanta. There was an earthquake, and you were caught in the citadel by falling stones.'

There was no lifting of the blankness in his gaze, no stirring of any emotion beyond uncertainty. 'An expedition? Backed by whom?'

'The Linden Foundation—which also owns this place. You were dig director. We'd only been there a couple of weeks.'

'Who else was on the team?'

She listed names, afraid to leave out Janine's in case he should later check. There was still no reaction, but for the first time it occurred to her to wonder what was going to happen if he should insist on returning to the dig when he was released from the clinic. Already the pitfalls were yawning, yet she found it impossible to turn back on her decision. Somehow she had to make him leave Peru. She would find a way.

'And you? he asked at length, watching her face. 'How is it you were with me on a dig?'

'I was resident artist,' she said. 'I took a course in archaeological draughtsmanship.'

'I remember you saying you were interested in doing that the first night we met,' he admitted. 'Only I don't ... I don't ...' He broke off, moving his head in confused fashion on the pillow. 'Obviously I changed my opinions after we were married.' His smile was faint. 'Or did you change them for me?'

Donna forced a smile of her own. 'We compromised. I was to share your work until the time we started a family.'

'Family?' For a moment something flickered deep down, but only for a moment. 'Sounds fair enough on the face of it. I want ... wanted children.'

'We can still have them.' Her tone was soft. 'Any time you like. Now that we're out of the Incanta dig we don't have to wait any longer.'

This time the look in his eyes was only too recognisable. 'Do you realise,' he said wryly, 'that I don't even remember our wedding night? I know you made me wait. I do remember the frustration.'

'It was worth it,' she said.

'Was it?' He studied her with speculation. 'Is it still?'

'More than ever.' If there had been a time for retreat it was long past. On impulse she put her face down to his and kissed him lingeringly on the lips, feeling his response with a sense of justification. 'I love you so much, Blake,' she whispered. 'You'll never know what I've been through waiting for you to wake up!'

His mouth was tender, eyes lit by an emotion she had longed to see. 'You've been sitting there a whole week?'

Oh, God, she thought, another trap! If she said yes it would only take a few casual words from any of the staff to prove her a liar, yet how to explain her reasons for not sticking close through the whole ordeal?

'Three days, to be exact,' she corrected after only a momentary pause. 'You were flown out from Incanta by helicopter along with the other injured in the party. I went back to Cuzco with the rest, then followed you down here on the first available flight.'

'You didn't feel I needed you all the way?' His tone was level but with an underlying note she could not ignore.

'I wanted to be with you, of course, but only the injured got taken out by air. I came as soon as I could.'

'I'm sure you did.' He lifted a hand and put his fingers to her lips, silencing her protests. 'I'm not criticising you. You must have gone through hell in all that mess! Was anyone killed?'

'No. You were the most seriously injured. I thought

you might even be dead before I got to you. It was . . .' Her voice broke, her head going down to his chest. 'Blake, let's go home. As soon as you're well enough to travel, I want to go home!'

'Where is home these days?' he asked, smoothing her hair. 'My work with your father must have finished a long time back. Did we stay on in England?'

Donna tensed, scarcely knowing how to answer that question. It wasn't going to be easy. None of it was going to be easy. But she was committed.

'My father died a few months ago,' she said. 'You were at Harvard until this Incanta expedition came up.'

'So you came back to America with me.' Blake sounded gratified. 'I'm sorry about your father. He was a fine man in many ways. Taking you away from him was a real struggle. I suppose most fathers are possessive about their daughters—especially where they're all he has.'

But at the time he was thinking of he wouldn't have realised just *how* possessive, acknowledged Donna numbly. 'I'd like to go back to England now,' she said, choosing her words with care. 'The Museum would take you like a shot.'

It was a moment or two before he responded. 'They may already have found a replacement for your father. Jobs like that are few and far between.'

'They hadn't up to a month or so ago. Clive Needham has been running the department, but he doesn't have the qualifications to take over on any permanent basis.' She lifted her head to look at him, trying to restrain her eagerness. 'At least give it a try, Blake. For me. I want our children to be born in our own country.'

His laugh was shaky but genuine. 'You're getting a little ahead of me! I still have to get to know my wife.' He pulled her down to him, kissing her with a passion astonishing in one so recently returned from the dead. 'I could make love to you right now, do you know that? Why don't you just lock that door over there and let me show you.'

'And set back your recovery by another week?' Smiling, she shook her head. 'It's a tempting offer, but I must decline. Dr Vallego would be shocked out of his mind!'

'Dr Vallego doesn't have two and a half years to catch up on.' Blake's eyes clouded again. 'God, it's hard to take in. There's so much I have to learn!'

'You need to rest,' she said, afraid of more questions to which she had no ready answers. She put a hand on the bellpush before he could protest. 'There's going to be plenty of time to talk later.'

'You'd better have it all lined up. Every last detail.' Despite all he could do to delay it reaction was setting in, his eyes growing heavier by the minute. 'Don't go away,' he murmured. 'Don't ever go away. I need you.'

Donna fought back tears as sleep finally claimed him—the healthy, healing sleep both body and mind could no longer resist. He had needed her two years ago, and what had she done to him? If only she had known then what she knew now. If only she could go back and wipe out the hurt she had inflicted!

And what of the hurt she might be piling up for them both in what she was doing right now? came the inevitable question. Every last detail, he had said. How was she going to supply two and a half years of lies? There were so many ways she could slip up, so many points to cover. Somewhere along the line she was going to give herself away, and then what would happen? Blake would never believe another word she said if he ever learned the truth. She should have told him from the first and taken a chance on his reaction. Perhaps in the circumstances he would have been willing to start again. Only she would never know, would she, because she had jumped in with both feet and made a mess of everything as usual. Would she never learn to think before she acted?

She pulled herself together with an effort as Dr Vallego came in. It was done now and no use bemoaning the fact. She had gone too far to go back.

'So he sleeps. Good.' The doctor took hold of the limp wrist, nodding his head in satisfaction as he timed the pulse. 'Fine and regular. When he awakens again he will be feeling much stronger.' He eyed Donna across the bed for a brief moment, a certain speculative look in his eyes. 'Forgive me for asking, but would you say there is any emotional cause for this lapse of memory on your husband's part?'

Right then she longed to tell him the truth, only she lacked the courage to admit to her deception. Suppose he insisted she make a clean breast of the whole thing to Blake when he woke? No, it wasn't possible. It just wasn't possible!

'None that I can think of,' she said, lifting a pair of veiled blue eyes to his. 'We have our differences, of course. What married couple doesn't?'

'Which indeed.' It was obvious that he was not totally deceived, but he made no attempt to press the subject. 'He should be allowed to sleep for as long as he needs. It would be a good time for you to take luncheon, and prepare yourself for your coming talk. He will want to know everything that has happened to the two of you during those lost years. Can you recall enough to satisfy him?'

'I can try,' she said. 'Is it all right if I just sit here until he does wake up? I don't really feel like eating.'

'No, it is not all right. You need sustenance. There will be someone here with Señor Mitchell the whole time. We shall not allow him to slip away again.'

Donna had to accept the edict, although the very thought of food choked her. Back in the room she had been allocated, she stood at the window looking out over the grounds where other patients walked or were pushed in wheelchairs along gravelled pathways. Blake's love was all she had to hang on to now; it was all she needed to hang on to. As soon as he was fit to leave the clinic they would take a flight home to England. In the meantime, there was no harm in putting out feelers with regard to her father's former position. The museum would not only be happy but downright grateful to have a director of Blake's standing on the staff. He knew as much of the ancient cultures as her father ever had. Even the work he had done at Incanta could be revised through her own notes and records, copies of which could be obtained through proper channels without giving anything vital away to anyone. Her main aim now was to ensure that the relationship between her and Blake would be strong enough to withstand the possible return of his memory. What she had to hope for was the time.

It was to be a further three days before Dr Vallego would pronounce his patient ready to leave his supervision, three days during which Donna became even more deeply enmeshed in the web of deceit she was weaving. There was one particularly sticky moment when Blake noticed her missing rings. She murmured something about the confusion after the earthquake, which semi-explanation he appeared to accept at face value. They could be replaced, he said. Remembering the diamond hoop and plain gold band lying in her jewellery box back at the London flat, she felt sick with guilt. There were a thousand and one things to which she hadn't given a thought; a whole host of stumbling blocks yet to be skirted.

Trying to anticipate them all was beyond her. She had to put her trust in her wits.

Such incidents apart, the time they spent together brought a steadily increasing rapport. The twelve years between them seemed to have shrunk, their minds more atuned. Physical frustration affected them both to an equal degree, yet circumstances hardly permitted indulgence of need.

In the end it was Blake who precipitated matters by declaring his intention of effecting his own discharge. Faced by a will stronger than his own, Dr Vallego gave in. With the moment of departure from the clinic upon them, perversely Donna wanted to stay. There was a kind of safety about the place, isolated as it was from the world outside. The problems to be dealt with were growing by the hour.

Blake himself came up with another in the taxi taking them to the downtown hotel where they were to spend the next couple of days.

'I gather we left most of our stuff back in Massachusetts,' he said out of the blue. 'What were our plans for after the dig—or didn't we get that far?'

'We never discussed it,' Donna answered truthfully. 'It was going to be a lengthy dig.' Her mind was racing, trying to stay one jump ahead. 'The apartment was rented furnished. There was no point in hanging on to it.'

'What about personal gear—clothing etcetera?' He laughed. 'From what I can remember of you before we were married the things you brought down here with you have to be the very tip of the iceberg! Did you store the rest?'

'Yes.' There was nothing else she could say. He was hardly likely to believe she had sold or given away every item of clothing apart from those in her suitcase and the dress she was wearing now. She had a wardrobe full of

clothes back in the London flat. Somehow they had to
become substitutes for the non-existent ones. The flat
itself was another problem which would not simply
disappear if she ignored it. She would have to write to
the landlords and tell them she was giving it up. The
furnishings went with it, thank heaven, but all her
personal possessions would have to be cleared. Perhaps
one of her friends could be persuaded.

The scheming stopped right there as her mind at last
acknowledged the sheer impossibility of what it was
proposing. The whole thing had been impossible from
the start. Only if they went to live entirely alone on a
desert island could she hope to keep Blake from
eventually learning the truth. The job at the museum,
for instance. Everyone in the department knew she had
been separated from Blake. Someone would be sure to
mention that fact, even if only by way of congratulations
on their reconciliation. Why hadn't she thought of that
point already, when it was staring her so baldly in the
face right now?

She knew why, of course. Because she had been
turning a deliberately blind eye to all but the immediate
questions, hoping that by some miracle everything
would fall into place. Only miracles didn't happen in
real life. She had got herself into this mess and she had
to get herself out of it. There was only one way: she
must tell Blake the truth.

'Hey!' His soft exclamation cut through the descending black cloud of despair. 'Why the look of gloom?'
He took her hand in his, running the ball of his thumb
across the swelling mound at the base of her own. 'We
have two days before we need to start thinking about
mundane matters,' he said, smiling into her eyes. 'Two
whole days and two whole nights—the honeymoon I
never had. We're going to forget everything else. All
we're going to be thinking of is each other.'

Forty-eight hours. The temptation was great. Would things really be any worse, Donna asked herself, if she kept up the masquerade for that length of time? Forget everything else, Blake had said, so why not? At least she would have something to hold in her memory if her confession elicited the anticipated reaction.

The hotel was large and modern, luxurious enough to please the most exacting tastes. Their suite was on the sixth floor, with a superb view out over the city to the mountains from the windows.

'We shan't be seeing much of that,' said Blake softly, coming up behind her as the outer door closed behind the bellboy. His hands came about her waist, his lips nuzzling the nape of her neck where her hair had fallen apart. 'Are you hungry now, or shall we eat later?'

She turned within the circle of his arms, reaching up to find his mouth in a kiss that held all her inner desperation. 'I'm only hungry for you,' she whispered. 'Take me to bed, Blake.'

They half closed the blinds in the bedroom to give a gentler light, undressing each other with leisurely intimacy, one garment at a time, feeling the tactile warmth of skin against skin, the hardness of muscle, the pliancy of limb. Stretched at her side on the satin covers, Blake spent whole moments simply rediscovering her body, stroking, exploring, lightly tracing every hill and valley, fingertips reverent in their passage. Donna had learned long ago to parade her nudity proudly before him, to exult in the ease with which she could rouse him to desire. Watching his eyes, listening to the deepening note of his breathing, she knew that the power had not deserted her; that just the sight and feel of her was all it took. There might even once have been a time when she would have let it be enough, taking everything and giving little in return. Only not now. Not ever again. She wanted to give him all he was giving her, to make him shudder with pleasure.

Instinct alone told her to wait, to let this man of hers set the initial pace. He was drawing out time to exquisite proportions, holding the two of them at a peak only inhuman self-control could maintain. When he finally moved her body beneath him she was beyond all rational thought, beyond everything but the longing, the yearning, the desperate need for release, taking him to her with eager hands, enveloping him within her, moving to this rhythm with ever-increasing wildness and abandon until they slid together over the summit and fell sheer into oblivion on the other side.

Food held little interest over those two tumultuous days and nights. They ate only when they had to, for sustenance alone, not bothering to dress beyond the casual donning of a loose robe, uncaring of what might be thought by those who delivered trays to their door. There were no questions asked, no lies told. What conversation they shared was centred on discovery of inner self, not outer irrelevancies.

For Donna it was a time of remembering, of re-learning all she had once so casually thrown away. Blake had taught her not only the ways of love but the moods of it too: passion; tenderness; daring, even humour. To laugh with love was not to laugh at it. The sharing was all.

For Blake himself there were no memories. Everything was new. Mentally he was prepared for the girl he had known; the girl he had married. What he found was a woman as awakened and aware as he was himself. There were times when she took him by surprise; times when he lost the command he held so dear.

'Where did you learn to be like this?' he murmured hoarsely on one occasion, and she laughed deep down in her throat.

'From you, my darling. From my own incomparable

sensualist of a husband who always knew exactly what he wanted, and how, and when—and taught me so well to please him.'

'You do please me,' he said. 'Oh, God, how you please me!' The arms about her were possessive, their strength a spur to her own emotions. 'How could I forget all this? How could any man forget! You're the stuff of dreams, Donna.'

It was a dream that had inevitably to end. The question of where they were to go from here needed an eventual answer. Blake was the one to pose it, albeit with reluctance.

'If you're keen on going back to England,' he said in the early hours of that final morning, 'we'll give it a try. A new start for a new man. I'll contact the faculty from London and get someone to clear things up in Cambridge. You'll have to fill me in on the details. The last thing I want is a whole load of explanations.'

She should have told him then, but her courage was not equal to the task. Just a few more hours, she told herself fiercely, stopping his mouth with a kiss.

They slept late after that final shattering union. By the time they had ordered and eaten breakfast and got themselves dressed it was already gone ten. They were flying to London via Miami, on flights booked by phone while they waited for room service. With the moment for decision upon her, Donna could find half a dozen reasons for delay. Get the journey over first, find a place to stay. She needed time to consider her approach to the subject. After what they had experienced together these past two days, Blake would surely understand her reasons for deceiving him. Had she told him the truth from the beginning that experience might never have been.

Blake asked for a taxi to be called before they left the suite. Their bill was ready and waiting at the desk.

Donna stood to one side while he paid it, idly watching the comings and goings in the lobby. The woman crossing purposefully towards the reception desk failed to register immediately with her. Only when Janine turned her head slightly and their eyes met did she come alive to the threat. It was as if the world suddenly stopped spinning.

CHAPTER NINE

BLAKE turned from the desk as Janine reached them, his eyes passing over her without recognition.

'That's it,' he said, taking Donna's arm. 'The taxi's waiting.'

'Blake?' His former colleague was looking at him uncomprehendingly. 'Blake, it's me—Janine. What on earth is wrong with you?'

His brows drew together, the hand under Donna's elbow tensing. 'I'm sorry,' he began, 'I'm afraid I don't . . .'

'This is Dr Meade,' Donna cut in with a total lack of emotion. 'She was—is on the Incanta dig. I thought you'd be back there by now,' she added to the other woman.

'Official delays. We leave at the weekend.' Her eyes were still on Blake, searching his face with a glimmer of understanding beginning to form. 'We heard you'd left the clinic, but they seemed reluctant to say much about your state of health, so I came down to find out for myself.' For the first time she switched her attention to Donna directly, her mouth tightening. 'You were supposed to be going straight back to England—or was that just an excuse?'

'Why should my wife go to England when I was here in Lima?' asked Blake, obviously at a complete loss.

'Your *wife*!' Janine was startled out of her customary composure. 'When did *that* happen?'

'I don't understand,' he said, frowning. 'If you were on the dig you must have known we were married.'

145

Her laugh sounded brittle. 'I was on the dig all right, but I can assure you I knew nothing of the kind.' She looked at Donna again, eyes narrowed. 'Supposing you tell me just what's going on?'

People were beginning to stare curiously at the three of them, sensing the tension. Donna could hear her heart thudding against her ribs, feel the sick defeat spreading through her. She made an effort to pull herself together, meeting Blake's questioning eyes with appeal in her own.

'I have to talk to you.'

He gazed at her in silence for what seemed an age, his regard slowly and subtly hardening as he read the guilt in her face. 'I think we'd better,' he said at length. 'You'll excuse us, Dr Meade.'

'Just a minute.' Janine was not about to let it go at that. 'Did something happen to your memory, Blake? Is that what this is all about?'

'Something happened to my memory, yes,' he agreed, still watching Donna with that same steely expression. 'I don't remember the dig, I don't remember the accident, and I'm afraid I don't remember you. Now, if you wouldn't mind . . .'

Donna could almost feel sorry for the archaeologist as they left her standing there. Blake moved beside her like a stranger, not touching her, not even glancing her way. At this hour of the morning the bar was only just opening for custom. He selected a table in a dim corner, waving away the waiter who started towards him.

'All right,' he said, 'let's have it. The whole story, Donna. And I want the truth!'

The truth. Where did she begin? She gazed at him numbly, gripped by the difficulties in making him understand. If he didn't remember his own attitude towards her these last few weeks how could she convince him of her own need to forget it?

'Our marriage only lasted six months,' she said at last. 'Six months together, that was. You blamed my father for breaking us up, only there was more to it than that.' She drew a ragged breath, dreading what had to come next. 'I found out I was pregnant and I didn't want to be—not then. Because my mind wasn't on what I was doing I walked under a car that same day. I—I lost the baby.'

The grey eyes were dark and unreadable. 'Are you trying to say we broke up because of that?'

'Not exactly, although it came into it.' Donna swallowed thickly. 'Blake, I'm not making excuses for myself . . . or I'm trying not to. I was in a state of mind where I didn't know what was most important to me any more. When you said you were going back to the States I just couldn't accept it. So you went without me.'

'And I can't accept that. Not the way it sounds.' He was clipped and unyielding. 'Whatever I might have felt about the baby I couldn't have just walked out and left you without one hell of a struggle. Not the way I feel . . . felt about you. There had to be other factors involved.'

'There were. My father was the main one. You said only a few weeks ago that he was jealous of you because you'd taken me away from him. I didn't agree with you then, but I've begun to see since that you could so easily have been right. He'd made plans, you see. Just for the two of us. He wanted me back.'

'And you were willing to go because you'd no feeling left for me?'

'No, that's not true!' She paused, desperately seeking the right words. 'It wasn't quite like that.'

'All right then, you never had any depth of feeling for me in the first place. Is that closer the mark?'

Donna closed her eyes momentarily, the hopelessness of it all swamping her. 'I suppose it has to be. Father always said I was confusing attraction with love. At the time he was probably right.'

'But now is different?'

'Yes. Oh yes!' She longed to reach out and touch the hand which lay clasped into a semi-fist on the table, but the coldness in his face stopped her. 'Blake, I'm two years older. I've learned a lot since then.'

'You hardly need to point that out,' he said. 'You've been proving just how much these past two days!'

'No!' It was cry of pure anguish, drawing a curious glance from the direction of the bar. 'You can't believe that. There hasn't been anyone else since you—not in any intimate sense. Everything we've been to each other here we were before.'

'Except that you're older now, and according to your own assessment, a different person. Two years of total abstinence hardly improves technique to the extent of the woman I've been sharing a bed with. You were as aware of my needs as if we'd made love every day of our lives!'

'It wasn't the first time since we parted,' she denied. 'We spent a whole night together in a cave after I got myself lost in the mountains not so long ago.'

'And?' He lifted a sardonic brow when she failed to answer. 'What happened after that?'

'You told me next morning that you'd had your revenge on me for all the pain I'd caused you.' Her voice was very low. 'You had too. You see, I'd fallen in love with you for real by then.'

'What a hard case I must have become.' He put up a slow hand to touch the light dressing still in place above his temple, eyes narrowing in seeming concentration. 'That apart, how is it you were on the dig in the first place if you didn't accompany me?'

'I already told you—resident artist. I was as shocked as you were when you arrived out of the blue the way you did.' Donna bit her lip at the blank expression in his eyes, remembering the circumstances of that unexpected arrival. 'John Brinkman was originally to direct the expedition. He broke an ankle just before he was due to leave for Lima, and you were asked to take over.'

'So John gave you the job?' He studied her for a lengthy moment, calculating the odds. 'I don't think so,' he said at last. 'He and I might not be professionally of the same mind, but I know him pretty well. There are dozens of archaeological artists with a hell of a sight more experience than you can have had. Why should he pick you?'

'My father's name . . .' she began, and saw his lip curl.

'Not good enough.'

'You didn't let me finish. My father's name drew his attention to the samples of my work that were sent to him. If he hadn't thought me good enough I'm quite sure it wouldn't have swayed him.'

'*You* sent him samples of your work?'

'No.' It had to come out, of course, but she knew what he was going to think. She forced herself to hold his gaze. 'The expedition's photographer was a friend of mine, and he submitted for me.'

'A friend?'

The intimation was exactly as she had anticipated. She shook her head. '*Just* a friend.' Conscience stirred her to qualify that statement. 'At least . . . well, we never slept together.'

'Then what exactly was the relationship?'

'He asked me to marry him.' Donna saw the tensing of the already hard jawline and hurried on, 'I wasn't in love with him. I only really got to know him since my father died. He was a . . . comfort.'

'I'm sure of it.' Blake gave her no time to reply. 'So what happened to that little affair? Did you leave him in Cuzco to come chasing down here after me?'

The lift of her shoulders bespoke her weariness. 'You sent him back before we reached Incanta. He had *soroche*.'

'And he went just like that without you?'

'We'd already agreed it wasn't going to work out between us.'

'Not when you already had a husband you'd suddenly realised you loved so deeply after all.'

'Don't mock me,' she said painfully. 'It didn't happen overnight. There were times during those weeks when you made me hate you. And if we're going to get on to past affairs of any kind, how about your own? You admitted to having a very physical one going with Janine Meade while the two of you were on expedition in Bolivia last year.'

'Really?' He sounded quite calm about it. 'I'll give myself top marks for taste. She's a very attractive woman. I know her by reputation, of course. That appears to go back before my trip to England. The Bolivian venture sounds intriguing. I trust we both took plenty of notes at the time.'

'Stop it!' Donna's teeth were clenched, her body rigid. 'Blake, you have to believe me. I followed you down here after you were injured because I had to be with you. When I realised you'd lost your memory I lost my head. I know it sounds crazy now, but I thought we could start again from scratch.'

'So you lied through your teeth about every damn thing. The apartment in Cambridge, the things we left there . . . God knows what else.' He was like a man without emotions, his tone level and chill. 'Why should

I believe you, Donna? Why should I believe a single word you tell me? Convince me.'

'I can't,' she said hopelessly. 'Not with words.'

'Not with the kind of action you've been giving me this last forty-eight hours either,' he retorted cruelly. 'Much as I enjoyed it, it only proves one thing. Still, a whole lot of marriages manage to scrape along on less.'

She gazed at him with new life stirring within her. 'Does that mean we're going to stay together?'

'It means,' he said, 'That I see no cause to turn my back on the kind of sexual gratification most men would give their eye teeth for. For the rest . . .' the shrug was meant to hurt '. . . we'll see how it goes.' He glanced at his watch. 'In the meantime, we have a plane to catch.'

Donna watched him get to his feet. She felt unable to move. 'You still intend going to England?'

'Isn't that where you wanted to go?' His lips twisted. 'It's about the only place where I'm not going to have to answer a lot of fool questions. A new start, you said. Where better than where it all began in the first place.'

'Blake,' she appealed desperately, 'rant at me, rave at me, do *anything*—just don't be this way! Less than two hours ago you told me you loved me.'

'I loved the girl from two and a half years ago,' he said hardily. 'You've kept me too mesmerised to think about the differences. Right now I don't even want you in the physical sense, though I'm sure that will pass once the shock starts to wear off.'

'And if I'm not willing to settle for that?'

'Oh, but you will. You need me to satisfy that appetite of yours.' He leaned over and drew her upright, lip curling at the entreaty in her eyes. 'Stop fooling yourself, Donna. You're not fooling me. I'm not complaining too much. I may have lost a few more illusions, but there are compensations.'

Not if she refused to go with him, Donna thought, and knew herself incapable. Blake was everything to her—and not just physically. As long as she stayed with him there was hope of recapturing what she had lost.

There was no sign of Janine out in the lobby. Faced with that brutal dismissal, Donna felt that she too would have decided enough was enough. The taxi they had ordered was gone, but another was soon procured. Moving away from the hotel, she wondered blindly if she would ever see this part of the world again. The land of the Incas had brought her little in the way of luck.

They landed in London at eight-thirty in the morning after a flight that for Donna at least had been far from restful. The warm and sunny weather lightened her mood a little. In sunshine nothing seemed quite as bad. She was here with Blake, and that was the main thing. There would be time to work at their relationship.

They had spoken little during the night. Apart from telling him about the flat, she had not attempted to fill in any detail of her life style these past few months since her father's death. The sale of the house, plus the balance of estate she had inherited under his will, had left her comfortably provided for. She had been able to afford one of the roomier conversions in Bloomsbury itself, and add her own personal touch to the décor.

Like all places left empty for any length of time, the rooms smelled musty. A pile of mail lay on the lobby mat. Blake picked it up for her, laying it on the nearby small table.

'Home, sweet home,' he commented with irony, looking in on the sizeable sitting room with its long, low sofa and scattering of chairs. 'First thing we need is a few windows opening. Do you have any coffee in?'

'I'm sure to have.' She moved towards the kitchen,

adding over her shoulder, 'The bedroom is back there, the bathroom next to it. Feel free.'

'Don't worry,' he said, 'I shall. Bring the coffee through there when it's ready, will you. I need to catch up on some sleep.'

Through in the kitchen Donna stood for a moment with closed eyes, willing herself to carry this through. Blake was still feeling the effects of shock, to say nothing of jet-lag. Things would be better after they had slept. They had to be better!

He was in the shower when she took the coffee in; she could hear the water gushing. He had not yet unpacked his suitcase, simply dumped it on the floor alongside her own. The bedroom looked warm and inviting in its gold and white scheme. Blake had taken off the dust sheet from the double bed and turned back the spread beneath, revealing the bare mattress in mute suggestion. Donna put down the tray and went to fetch bedding from the closet.

The water had stopped running by the time she had finished making up the bed. A moment later he came through, wearing nothing but a towel slung about his hips. His hair was damp, the dressing removed. His wound was healing well, the scarring due to fade a great deal with time, they had been told at the clinic. She searched the grey eyes for some sign of change in attitude, but there was none that she could see. Tiredness had to mask emotion, she told herself. She felt worn out too. Once they had slept they would talk this whole thing out on a rational basis.

Blake drank his coffee sitting on the edge of the bed. 'Are you coming?' he asked when she got up from the cane chair to deposit her own mug back on the tray.

'We need food,' she said. 'I thought I'd shop first and sleep later.'

'We'll both shop later.' He put down his mug and

casually removed the towel, lying down to pull the sheet over his waist. The eyes meeting hers were cynical. 'I told you the shock would wear off. Come to bed, Donna. If we have nothing else, we still have this.'

She stayed where she was, looking at him helplessly. After a moment he got up again and came over to her, swinging her up into strong arms to carry her back to the bed and toss her lightly on to the mattress. He had her shirt unbuttoned and his fingers on the buckle of her belt before she found the strength of mind to stop him, putting her hand over his.

'What do you think I'm going to be?' she demanded. 'A commodity for your use? No matter what I've done, I'm not going to be treated like a—a whore!'

'I've no intention of treating you like a whore,' he said, totally unmoved. 'You're my wife, and I want you. If you don't want me, tell me now before it's too late.' He was watching her eyes, now he moved his free hand to her breast, smiling to see the leap of response. 'This is one aspect of you I have complete confidence in,' he murmured. 'We have to make the most of what we have. You'd agree with that?'

'Yes. No!' She moved her head on the pillow in agonised indecision. 'I don't *know*!'

'Well, I do.'

He leaned down and put his lips to hers, the demand irresistible. In spite of herself, Donna started kissing him back, feverishly seeking the man within the hardened shell. He finished undressing her without further objection on her part, the irony plainly visible about his mouth and eyes as he looked at her.

'Having this returned to me has to be a bonus of sorts. The rest I can live without.'

'I love you,' she whispered despairingly, and saw the smile harden anew.

'So you keep telling me. One of these days you might

even convince me again. Until then I'll settle for what I know is real.'

It was real enough, she thought, feeling the desire surging through her as he lowered his head to her body. With or without love, she wanted him so much it was like a pain inside her. One of these days she *would* convince him. She really would. In the meantime she could only give way to mutual needs.

The directorship at the museum was still open. Blake's application was received and acted upon with a speed of decision that had him installed within a week. Meeting her father's former colleagues for the first time in almost seven months, Donna steeled herself against the obvious curiosity, accepting the anticipated congratulations on her reconciliation with Blake with smiling reserve. Let them wonder. It was no one's business but their own.

Gradually life began to settle into a pattern. Blake had sent to Harvard for his books and personal items, and seemed content enough on the surface. They talked together like sane and sensible people, went to meetings and social gatherings together, even shared the same theatrical and musical tastes. It was only in intimacy that the missing element was apparent. Blake was passionate, he was generous, he was never disinclined, but the tenderness that had been so much a part of their time together in the Lima hotel was a thing of the past. Donna tried to tell herself that it would return, and knew she was living in a fool's paradise. She had killed all softness and gentleness in him. They might stay together for the rest of their lives, but it would never be the same again. The loss went deep.

Conscience had forced her into trying to contact Graham, only to discover he was out of the country on another job. His return in August coincided with the weekend they were scheduled to entertain several members of the department and their partners to a buffet supper in celebration of a completed project. Finding him at the door halfway through the evening was a shock of some proportion.

'I only got in this afternoon,' he said. 'My answering service said you'd tried to get in touch.' His glance went beyond her to the opened door to the sitting room. 'Having a party?'

'Kind of.' Resignedly she stepped back. 'You'd better come in, Graham. I have a lot to tell you, and it can't be said on the landing.'

Blake came out from the other room as she closed the outer door, a wine bottle in his hand. 'Did you see the other corkscrew . . .' he began, then stopped abruptly as his eyes fell on the newcomer. Realisation was swift. 'Hallo there,' he said. 'You look as if you've been enjoying rather more sun than we've had here.'

'I was in Israel for the last couple of months,' replied the younger man. He was doing everything he could to conceal his feelings and not succeeding very well. 'So the two of you got back together again. Congratulations.'

'Thanks.' Blake's tone was dry. 'Come on in and have a drink. You might find it interesting. No, I insist,' he added as Graham opened his mouth on an obvious excuse. 'We were all on the same team, even if it was for a limited period. You recovered from the *soroche* fairly fast, I hope? Sometimes it can leave after-effects.'

Graham glanced a little helplessly in Donna's direction and gave in. 'I'm fine, thanks.'

Introductions took up quite a time. By the time Donna managed to get a word alone the evening was almost over.

'I'm sorry if you got embroiled,' she said, sitting down beside him on the sofa. 'Shop talk tends to carry the whole conversation at these affairs. The Israeli job sounded fascinating. A *tell* has so much history buried in it—all those different levels.' She paused, eyeing him questioningly. 'Were you telling Blake the truth earlier? You haven't suffered repercussions from the altitude sickness?'

He shook his head. 'None to speak of. My G.P. doesn't seem too concerned about the heart murmur, providing I take things at a reasonable pace.' He paused, his face reflecting inner disturbance. 'How about you, Donna? Are you happy?'

'Of course.' She said it lightly. 'Don't I look it?'

'You look wonderful,' he responded with warmth. 'You never looked anything else.' He paused again, studying her with tilted head. 'But there's something different about you. I'm not sure what.'

'I've aged three months since you saw me last,' she said, laughing. 'In January I'll be twenty-four! Just think of it—almost my quarter century!'

'I know what it is,' said Graham, ignoring the latter sally. 'You're trying too hard. You're working to convince me that everything in the garden is lovely. Why, Donna? Why do you feel the need?'

The laughter gave way to a rueful little smile. 'You always could see through me.'

'That doesn't answer the question.'

She shrugged. 'It's nothing anyone can do anything about.'

'Blake?'

'Yes, but not in any way I can discuss. It's something I've only myself to blame for.' Deliberately she lightened her tone again. 'I'll work it out.'

'All right,' he said. 'Only just remember, if you ever need a friend I'll still be here.'

'I'll remember.' She felt a swift pang. Graham had loved her once, and perhaps still did. Would he have reacted the way Blake was reacting to the same situation? It seemed doubtful on the face of it, yet how could one tell? Love was an emotion only matched in strength by hate, the dividing line no more than a hair's breadth. She had crossed it herself on so many occasions these past months. Why should Graham be an exception?

'Tell me about yourself,' she said, pushing the whole fraught subject to the back of her mind. 'What do you have planned next?'

'I'm not sure,' he admitted. 'I've a couple of small jobs lined up between now and Christmas, but nothing out of the ordinary. By the way,' he added as if in sudden recollection, 'guess who I saw at Heathrow this afternoon?'

Donna shook her head. 'I can't imagine.'

'Dr Meade, no less.'

Something in her went cold. 'Coming or going?'

'Oh, coming. Most definitely coming. She'd just got in from Lima. It seems they left the Incanta dig some weeks ago, but she's been working with Juan Prieto on the cataloguing. She said something about the Museum running an exhibition of Incanta finds. I suppose Blake will be handling the details now he's head of department. They must have been very glad to get him.'

'Yes, they were.' Donna's mind was racing ahead as always, covering the implications. If Janine was already in the country then arrangements for the exhibition must already be well under way. Why hadn't Blake mentioned it to her? Why would he want to keep such a thing to himself? The answer stared her in the face. Janine, of course. He might not remember his previous affair with her, but it was almost certain that he recalled the meeting in Lima in perfect detail. A very attractive woman, he had called her. Perhaps he had his own reasons for wanting to keep her presence strictly to himself.

She had to stop this, she thought numbly. She was reading far too much into far too little. Yet was she? If the exhibition was to be staged then it might well include some of her own drawings on site—unless the substitute had turned out to be appreciably her superior in the art. In any case, she had a right to be involved. She had *been* there. What was more, unlike Blake, she could actually remember it.

She stayed with Graham the rest of the evening, turning a blind eye to the needs of her guests. If they were short of anything Blake would supply it. He was very good at demand and supply. Graham was among the last to leave. She saw him to the door herself, lingering on the landing to watch him down the stairs. There went the life she could have had, the man she could have loved. It wouldn't have been as physically satisfying as the one she led with Blake, but at least her emotions would never have undergone the same strain. There was a lot to be said for moderation.

Blake locked the outer door on the final guest before coming through to the kitchen where Donna was loading glasses and china into the dishwasher.

'Leave that till morning,' he said from the doorway. 'It's late.'

She answered without looking up from her task. 'I prefer to do it tonight.'

'And *I* prefer not!' He was across the floor before she could turn, whipping her round to face him with a hand like iron. There was anger in his eyes, a too familiar tension in the line of his jaw. 'You've already come close to making me lose my temper in front of the whole department. Try me any further tonight and I'm not going to be answerable for what I'll do to you! Do you understand that—or do you need showing?'

'I understand perfectly.' She was determined not to let him browbeat her. 'Do as I say but not as I do!'

His expression altered subtly, eyes narrowing. 'What's that supposed to mean exactly?'

He still had hold of her wrist, fingers unyielding. She leaned her weight against the sink behind her, not taking her eyes from his face. 'Why didn't you tell me about the exhibition?'

Whatever his reaction, it certainly wasn't guilt. 'It didn't come up,' he said. 'Who told you?'

'Graham. He saw Janine Meade at the airport this afternoon.' Her tone took on mockery, soft and deliberate. 'You do remember Janine, don't you? The blonde in Lima? You have a weakness for blondes, she once told me.'

'So that's it.' He sounded mocking himself. 'The jealous little wife! How touchingly appropriate.'

'Why shouldn't I be jealous?' she demanded. 'Wasn't that what made *you* so furious when I spent so much time with Graham tonight?'

'You were neglecting our guests,' he responded with control. '*That's* what made me furious. As for Dr Meade, she happens to be acting for the Peruvian government in checking security arrangements over here. The gold they found is worth a great deal of money—to say nothing of the priceless value of the figurines themselves. Naturally they need to be assured that display conditions meet their requirements.'

'Why Janine? Why not Juan Prieto himself?'

'How the hell would I know? If she managed to persuade the officials over there that she was the person for the job in preference to one of their own, then good luck to her! She must be quite a woman.'

'Oh, she is! *All* woman, I think you'd call her. Blonde, beautiful, clever—you wouldn't credit her gifts! And generous with them too, especially where other women's husbands are concerned. You really ought . . .'

Blake cut her off right there, his hands digging into

her shoulders as he shook her long and hard. Her hair was tumbled about her face when he finally desisted, her lower lip caught between her teeth. She turned her head away from him as she gained control of herself, hating the thought of his seeing the hurt in her eyes.

'Violence is just about your level,' she got out through the dryness in her throat. 'When do you start hitting me?'

'Don't think I haven't been tempted.' His own breathing was ragged, the hands he had dropped clenched into fists as he moved away from her. 'You're driving me insane, do you know that?'

'No more than you're driving me.' Her voice was thick. 'We live together, we sleep together, we make love ... if that's what it should really be called ... and we don't even like each other most of the time. Why don't we just call it a day, Blake?'

It took him a while to answer that one, his back turned to her, his bearing rigid. 'I'll decide when *I* want to call it a day, thanks. If we split up you're going to have to take the initiative.'

'It's my flat,' she protested. 'Why should I be the one to go?'

'Now you're the one with the memory problem. I took over the lease, yes?' He glanced at her when she failed to make any comeback, his expression impossible to define. 'Think about it.'

'Blake.' Her voice was low, her eyes averted. 'Has it ever occurred to you to wonder why else I would have lied to you at all if it wasn't because I was so afraid of losing you again?'

'It never occurred to me that there might be any other explanation,' he said. 'What I would and do dispute is your depth of feeling for me. If you'd loved me the way you say you did you'd have been honest with me.'

'And if I had? Would you have been able to ignore the fact that I hurt you so badly in the past?'

'Without being able to remember it, there was every chance. You didn't give me that chance.'

'Then give me one. Let me near you again.' She was trying not to plead. 'Do you really believe I'm capable of acting the kind of emotion we shared those two days?'

'You're capable of many things,' he declared without inflection. 'Self-deception among them, I shouldn't wonder. I'm going to bed. You please yourself.'

As honeymoons went, Donna reflected painfully as he left her, this one was definitely over.

CHAPTER TEN

JANINE paid her first call a week later, turning up at the flat one afternoon when Blake was still at the museum.

'I thought we should renew our acquaintance considering we're going to be seeing quite a lot of each other over the next few weeks,' she said smoothly over coffee. 'I'm being paid to keep my eye on things during the entire run of exhibitions here in England. Birmingham have already applied to be next in line. It should prove an interesting year.'

'I'd have thought a pretty boring one,' Donna responded, and received an oblique glance from cool green eyes.

'Dependent on the venue to a degree. If others prove as helpful and considerate as Blake and his staff have been I shan't have any complaints. Are you coming to the opening?'

'I wouldn't miss it,' Donna forbore from pointing out that she had not yet been told the date. 'Did you find conditions very difficult when you got back to Incanta?'

'More so than they had been. We managed.' The archaeologist paused, a hint of purpose in her regard. 'You know, I have to give you credit. You had me completely foxed from the start. You must have been mad if you imagined you could keep up the act after Blake lost his memory, though. Even if I hadn't let the cat out of the bag, someone or something else would have done. You're lucky he stayed with you.'

'Aren't I?' Donna made no attempt to conceal the irony in her voice. 'Did Blake suggest you should come to see me?'

'No, that was my own idea.' Janine laughed. 'As a matter of fact, I doubt if he'd be too keen. You know what men are—they imagine women only have to get together to start telling all.' The pause once more was timed. 'I gather the two of you may be undergoing some marital strain.'

Donna froze. 'Did he tell you that?'

'Not exactly. I'm reading between the lines. It's hardly surprising. What you both need is taking out of yourselves.'

'What would you suggest?' Donna asked sweetly. 'An affair apiece?'

'Don't knock it. A lot of marriages benefit from a little infidelity.' Janine made a sudden impatient gesture. 'Look, I didn't come here to spar with you. Believe it or not, I'm trying to help.'

'Why?' The question was unemotional. 'Do you tend to worry about all your ex-lovers this way?'

'So you know about that.' Janine sounded more amused than anything. 'He doesn't remember it now, so he must have told you before the quake. Naughty of him!' She put down the coffee cup with a decisive movement. 'All right, cards on the table. I want your husband, and if I think there's any chance of getting him I'll take it. I could share his work the way you never could.'

Donna stared at her, hardly able to credit the supreme ego. 'Except that he doesn't happen to believe in husband and wife working together,' she said, and saw the smile come and go.

'Marriage isn't what I'm talking about. I'm not one for tying shackles on a man, or for wanting them tied on me. Blake was happier without you, he would be again.' She came to her feet, arrogant in her certainty. 'Think about it. Don't bother to see me out—the door isn't hard to find.'

Donna sat looking fixedly ahead as the archaeologist left. Janine had a point. Blake would be happier without her in the long run. As for herself? Well, she could scarcely be more miserable, could she? It had been a week since he had even made love to her. With that gone what did they have left worth hanging on to?

It was gone five before she remembered that they were supposed to be going out to dinner that evening. She contemplated crying off on the pretext that she was feeling unwell, but the effort entailed in living out that part seemed greater than simply getting ready and going.

She was in the shower when Blake came home around six-thirty. She donned a towelling robe to go back to the bedroom, entering quietly to find him sitting on the bed with his head down and his fingertips slowly massaging his temple.

'Just tired,' he said when she asked him if anything was wrong. His glance moved over her without altering expression. 'Finished in there?'

'Yes.' She passed him to open a drawer and take out fresh undies, wondering how he would react if she told him about Janine's visit today. Not that she had any real intention; it would make little difference to her position. 'You'd better hurry,' she said. 'We have a good forty to fifty-minute drive out to Ashley—unless you'd rather I called and told the Portmans you don't feel up to it?'

'I said I was tired,' he retorted brusquely, 'not incapable. If you need proof of that come on over here.'

Every instinct in her leapt to the invitation, but pride was stronger. 'We don't have time,' she said, 'even if I had the inclination. You seem to think you only have to snap your fingers to have me jumping through hoops!'

Blake was behind her before she heard him move, spinning her round to find her mouth in a kiss that had nerve and sinew taut as a drum, his hands running inside the robe with familiarity and possession. He let her go as swiftly as he had caught her, turning away while she was still drawing breath. 'You're right, we don't have the time. It will save.'

Swine, she thought achingly. He had done that on purpose, just to show her who was in charge. But at least it was better than being ignored. Anything was better than that!

She wore a black velvet skirt and white silk blouse for the evening, complementing Blake's own black and white. He was quiet in the car driving out of town, though the anger appeared to have dissipated. Once or twice she saw his brows draw together as if in concentration—or in pain; she wasn't sure which. To ask would be to invite another short, sharp answer, she decided, and left well alone.

Alec Portman was an old friend of her father's, and nothing to do with the museum. He and his wife had known Donna since she was a child, although this was the first time she had seen them since the funeral. The familiar, lovely old house just outside the village felt almost like home. Had her own marriage been stable, this was the kind of place she would have liked herself, she reflected wistfully while they waited for the bell to be answered.

Mary Portman greeted her with genuine pleasure, extending the same welcome to Blake.

'We were visiting our son in New Zealand at the time of the wedding,' she said frankly, 'and of course the two of you had parted before we came home, but I'm really happy that you got back together again. Donna needs someone to look after her, you know. She's not nearly as independent as she likes to think she is.' The last with a sly little chuckle as she saw Donna's expression. 'Come and have a drink and meet everyone. I think you're the last to arrive.'

There were four other invited couples, making a round total of twelve in all. Seated in the high-ceilinged dining room, Donna concentrated on her immediate neighbours and tried not to look at Blake across the oak refectory table between two attractive, intelligent and only slightly middle-aged women who seemed to enjoy competing for his attention. If she had a real marriage with a man who loved and trusted her, she wouldn't need to be jealous, she told herself in mitigation. So many women found Blake a draw, it followed that there had to be some to whom he was equally attracted. Janine was only one case in point. How did she know there weren't others?

One of the other male guests had also been initially introduced by the title of Doctor. It was only on falling into conversation with him later in the drawing room that Donna realised he was actually a doctor of medicine.

'I'm not local,' he said. 'My wife and I are spending a week's holiday with the Portmans. We met them last year when their car broke down right outside my surgery door. They finished up staying the night while they waited for it to be repaired, and we've gone on from there. You've known them both a long time, I understand?'

'Most of my life,' Donna acknowledged. 'I used to call Mary Aunt.'

'Until you grew up and became a married woman,' he smiled. 'Your husband is a very clever man. I've read his *People of the Sun*. Did you have a hand in that at all?'

'No,' she said, 'it was all his own work.' She added levelly, 'We were parted at the time.'

'Ah,' he nodded sagely. 'Marriage demands adjustment, from both sides. It's good to hear of one couple who managed to make it back together again. You'll be all the closer for it.' He paused, eyes resting on the man seated at the far side of the room talking with another couple. 'Tell me,' he added, 'how did he come by the scar on his forehead? It looks as if he might have been struck by some heavy object.'

'He was,' she said, and explained the bare details.

'Three months ago,' he mused thoughtfully. 'Does he suffer from headaches at all?'

Donna laughed and tried to pass the moment off. 'He wouldn't tell me if he did. Why?'

'I noticed at dinner that he occasionally put a hand to the spot as if he was experiencing some discomfort, but I may have been misreading the gesture. Have you noticed anything untoward yourself?'

Donna looked at him for a long moment in silence, her pulses jerking. 'I caught him holding his head earlier this evening,' she said at length, 'but he swore he was only tired.'

'Then that's probably what he was.' The tone was reassuring. 'All the same, it might not be a bad idea to persuade him to see his physician. Just for a check-up, you know.'

Donna spent the rest of the evening surreptitiously watching Blake, relieved when he showed no further sign of disturbance. Even so, the advice she had received carried enough weight to stay in her mind, eliciting a cautious enquiry when they were on their way home.

'Did your headache go off?'

'What headache?' he asked without taking his eyes from the floodlit road ahead.

'The one you had earlier when you came home. You were holding your head when I came from the bathroom.'

'Oh, that.' His tone was dismissive. 'It was nothing— atmospherics, probably. I enjoyed tonight.'

'So I noticed.' Donna tried to make the comment light and jocular, but suspected she failed miserably.

His response left her in no doubt. 'If you're going to start that business again I'll put you out of the car to walk it off. You don't own sole rights, Donna. Not to anything!'

'Who am I sharing with?' she demanded, losing all sense of moderation. 'Janine?'

The tyres skidded on loose gravel at the side of the road as Blake brought the car to an abrupt stop. Mouth grim, he reached across her and opened the door. 'Go on, get out! I've had about as much as I'm going to take from you tonight!'

She slid out of the seat without a word, high heels slipping in the gravel as she slammed the door in his face. Without waiting for the car to move off, she started to walk, head held high. The control was surface only. Inside she felt as shaky as a leaf in a high wind, her heart thudding sickeningly against her ribs. It quickened even further when she heard the sound of a door opening again, but she refused to turn round to the fast approaching footsteps.

Blake looked at the end of his tether, his teeth clenched so that the skin showed white about his mouth. Taking her by the wrist in a grip that hurt like fire, he dragged her back to the car and almost threw her into her seat, before moving back to his own. Putting the vehicle into motion again, he burned rubber with the force of acceleration.

Donna waited several moments before saying defensively, 'You were the one who told me to get out.'

'I know what I told you, damn you!' The anger was still seething in him, knuckles tensed where they gripped the wheel. 'Just shut up!'

It would have been sheer folly to defy that advice. Donna sat tight as he drove fast and furiously through the night. She felt no fear of the crash which seemed imminent. There was no feeling at all, just the dull realisation that they couldn't go on like this.

Blake slowed down as his temper cooled, but he still didn't speak. They reached home shortly after twelve-thirty. Donna went straight up to the flat while he garaged the car. She was in the bedroom when he came in.

'One of these days you'll make me do something I'll regret,' he said, tossing his key-ring on to the dressing table and starting to empty his pockets. 'What is it you want?'

'Trust,' she responded, not taking her eyes from the mirror and the brush in her hand.

His laugh came short. 'The way you trust me?'

'It's a different thing.'

'I fail to see why.'

'You don't *want* to see why! I'm the only culprit. Isn't that the way you look at it?' She put down the brush with an unsteady hand, watching him through the mirror. 'Perhaps if you'd allowed me a little individuality from the first we'd never have broken up at all.'

'And pigs might fly?' He took off his dinner jacket and slung it over a chair, ripping the studs from his shirt cuffs with savage force. 'Leave it alone, Donna. Just leave it alone!'

She bit down hard on the retort even now rising in her throat. Anger wasn't going to get them anywhere. She would leave it alone all right. She would leave *him* alone. There were hotels she could go to. First thing in the morning she would move out.

The resolution lasted until they were in bed with the lights out and their backs turned on each other. She couldn't leave him, she acknowledged painfully. What price her professed love if she could so easily give it up? Her body craved him even now. If physical expression was all he could offer her then why not accept it? She could always continue to hope for better things some day.

His back remained rigid when she rolled over towards him, but his breathing told her he wasn't asleep. He was wearing the bottom half of a pair of pyjamas, an innovation dating back over just the last few nights. She had donned a nightdress herself for the first time in months; the material twisted as she moved, wrapping itself about her legs. She slipped down the thin straps to press her bare breasts against the muscular back, sliding an arm over his waist with a faint sigh.

'Don't shut me out, Blake—not this way. I want you so much!'

There was no immediate response. He seemed almost to be holding his breath. When he did speak it was on a note so low she could scarcely hear him. 'Go to sleep, Donna. It isn't the time.'

'Then make it the time!' she said fiercely. 'Depriving me isn't going to do you much good either. Do you want me to crawl—to tell you I can't live without you? All right, so I can't live without you. Make love to me, Blake. It's all we have that's worth anything! Make love to me, damn you!'

He caught her wrist, flinging it aside as he came over towards her. The hands pinning her down into the pillows were savage, his face set in lines she didn't recognise. 'I *want* to make love to you,' he gritted. 'For God's sake, what do you think I'm made of? I'm impotent, you blind little fool! I can't make it any more. I haven't been able to make it for the last week. Now will you get to sleep and stop bothering me!'

Donna lay gazing at him in horror, not even feeling the pain of his grip as she absorbed the agony of mind behind the grim fury of the words. For any man to be forced into such an admission would be bad enough, for one of Blake's capacity a sentence of death would be preferable. She didn't know what to say, how to cope. He needed help of some kind, it was obvious, but where did one start?

'Are you sure?' she whispered lamely. 'A week isn't long.'

'It's been a lifetime.' He rolled over on to his back, lying with eyes fixed on the ceiling. 'Of course I'm sure. I don't need to go into physiological detail, do I?'

'No.' Donna lay still, trying to bring her mind to bear on the moment and not skitter ahead. When she spoke again it was with care. 'You haven't let me near you this last week. Perhaps . . .'

'Perhaps nothing.' His tone was rough. 'And I don't want a debate over it either.'

'You can't shut me out of this,' she protested. 'I won't let you!' She paused again, frantically scanning the possibilities. 'Blake, these headaches you've been having—could they be something to do with it?'

His laugh sounded brittle. 'That would be a new twist! The headaches are a result, not a cause.'

'You can't know that for certain without medical advice. Dr Norris at the Portmans' tonight was of the opinion that you should have a check-up.'

He said softly, 'What did you tell him?'

'Nothing very much. He noticed your scar and asked me how it happened. He said he'd seen you putting your hand to it as if you were in pain, and suggested it might be a good idea to let someone take a look at you.' She added hurriedly, 'I didn't mention your memory loss.'

'Thoughtful of you!'

The silence stretched. 'So?' she ventured at last. 'What about it?'

'There's nothing wrong with my head,' he said. 'And

it's going to be a long time before I start looking for outside help. I realise there's little to hold you in the circumstances. If you want to call it a day I'll go along.'

'No!' She came up on one elbow in swift emphasis. 'Do you really think I'd even consider doing that?'

'Pity is the last thing I want,' he flung at her. 'I know you too well, Donna. You can no more live without than I can!'

'There's more to love than sexual fulfilment,' she said after a moment. 'Perhaps this is the one way I'm going to be able to prove it to you.'

It was impossible to read his expression. When he did answer it was on an unemotional note. 'Let's leave it for now, shall we!'

She would dearly have loved to just put her arms about him and hold him, but she daren't make the move. Comfort of that kind was not what he sought. She had to tread with care if she wanted their marriage to remain intact. And she did want it. Life without Blake's lovemaking was infinitely preferable to total loss. Only he had to be persuaded to seek help for his own sake. Shorn of his virility he would feel himself only half a man, and what that would do to him was not to be contemplated.

Treading carefully became a habit with her over the days following. Every word, every gesture was examined for flaws before use. If Blake recognised her hesitation for what it was he made no mention of it. They were both of them walking a tightrope, with little leeway for error.

The exhibition opened to capacity crowds and a good press. Seeing it for the first time, Donna was fascinated to learn of the amount of excavation which had taken place after the earthquake. The latter had, in fact, revealed a series of underground chambers containing a great many artefacts of importance—among them a

fine collection of weaponry. Donna's own scale plan of
the site prior to disturbance was shown alongside the
later one for comparison. Several of her drawings and
written recordings were also in use. Studying them
again, she wondered why she felt no particular urging
towards a renewal of her career. It was as if the trauma
of that cataclysmic few weeks had driven all such
ambition from her mind.

Janine made her position felt in a manner which left
no one in any doubt as to who was in charge where the
exhibits were concerned. Blake seemed not to object to
the usurping of his own authority, treating Janine with
a   professional   deference   Donna   for   one   found
unmerited. The woman was not his equal, and never
would be. Even allowing for his forgotten years, he was
still the oracle where Inca lore was concerned.

There was a celebration party at the end of the first
week. Already Janine was talking of persuading the
Foundation to back a further expedition in search of
the 'City of Light' depicted in ideographic form on the
ceremonial vessels found at Incanta. She wanted Blake
with her as co-director, an offer to which he had not as
yet made any concrete reply. If he did go, Donna had
promised herself, she was going with him, if only in
protection. Janine must never be allowed to discover
the secret he so bitterly concealed. It was enough that
one woman knew.

The fact that she did know was slowly and
insidiously turning him against her, that she was
beginning to realise. Sometimes he could barely bring
himself to be in her company. Driving to the museum
tonight they had exchanged no more than a couple of
words, and those of a purely general nature. On arrival
he had appeared only too ready to turn her over to the
care of a colleague and involve himself with others.

Janine was sticking close, her arm tucked in intimate

fashion through his as they chatted with a group of people over by the weaponry display. Donna tried not to let wandering attention betray her thoughts to her own companions, but suspected she had been less than successful when one of the other women in the group asked somewhat bitchily if she found it anything of a strain living up to such a brilliant husband.

'Two brilliant minds in the family would be one too many,' she said on a light note. 'I prefer to bask in reflected glory.'

'With tongue tucked firmly into cheek,' chuckled the assistant curator, who had known Donna a long time. 'Having your work on show here proves you're no dumb blonde!'

Just a lonely one, Donna conceded, forcing a smile. And scheduled to be so for a long time, the way things were going.

The party ran its course the way such affairs were wont to do, with people wandering from group to group, glass in hand and bright remark on lip. As wife of the director, Donna performed her duty to the best of her ability, making sure everyone was adequately entertained. She first missed Blake around eight-thirty when people were beginning to drift away to follow plans for the rest of the evening, but thought nothing much of it until she realised that Janine was also conspicuous by her absence.

Try as she might to ignore the fact, the coincidence became too much for her in the end. Blake's office was down the rear corridor. There was no light showing, but the door was sufficiently ajar for her to hear the lowered voices from within. Without pause for reflection, she pushed the door wider and reached in a hand to switch on the light, looking with blank unemotionalism at the two only now breaking apart over by the desk. The expression on Blake's face was hard to define. Not guilt, for certain. Janine left her in no doubt at all. The smile was pure triumph.

'Caught in the act!' she exclaimed, sounding anything but sorry. 'I'm not sure quite what to say.'

'I'll say one thing for you,' Donna returned levelly. 'You leave no stone unturned! Carry on, both of you. I'll be at the flat when you're through, Blake.'

She was gone before either of them could speak.

CHAPTER ELEVEN

It was over an hour before Blake returned to the flat. Donna was waiting for him in the sitting room, the television switched on for company, although she could not have said which programme she was supposed to be watching.

Blake walked over and turned off the set, standing in front of it with hands thrust deep into pockets as he looked at her expressionlessly. 'So let's have it.'

She gazed back at him with rigid control. 'There's only one question I need answering. Are things any different with Janine?'

It seemed to take him a long time to reply. Watching his eyes she could almost sense the conflict within. When he did speak it was with a clipped delivery as if he wanted to get it over quickly. 'Yes, they are. I'm sorry, but I had to know.'

'I see.' There was no feeling as yet. That would come later. 'In that case, there isn't much point in carrying on, is there?'

'No,' he agreed. 'Not much point at all.' He moved abruptly, turning away towards the door. 'I'll move out to a hotel for the present.'

Donna made no attempt to argue that decision. It was quite obvious that he couldn't wait to leave. No doubt he had already made his arrangements with Janine. And why not? The other woman had given him back the manhood she herself had apparently taken away. The reasons why were not important any more. Understanding the problem would not bring him back to her. This time their marriage was over for good.

She was still sitting in the same position when Blake came back to the room. He had changed from the dark suit into slacks and suede jacket, his hair ruffled as though he hadn't even bothered to run a brush over it after drawing on the lightweight sweater. Donna watched his mouth as he spoke, remembering the feel of those firm lips on hers, the murmured words in the night. A part of her wanted to reach out and cling, to beg him to stay, but pride was stronger.

'Are you listening?' he asked with brusque inflection. 'I said I'll collect the rest of my things some other time. Naturally I'll continue to pay the rent for this place.'

'We can discuss that sort of thing later,' she said huskily. 'Right now I'd just like you to go, Blake.'

Even then he seemed to hesitate, jaw tight and set. It wasn't until the outer door finally closed behind him that Donna could bring herself to move, rising stiffly to her feet to turn on the television again. Some time soon the pain was going to hit, and hit hard; for the moment she simply felt numb. To hear voices and see people at least created an illusion of normality. She would cling to it as long as she was able.

Blake rang the following afternoon, sounding stilted over the line. They had to get things sorted out on a proper legal footing, he said without preamble. He had made an appointment to see a solicitor for eleven the next morning. Was she prepared to accompany him in order to speed matters along?

Donna agreed levelly, putting down the receiver on his promise to pick her up at the flat with a hand that remained quite steady. She had fought a hard battle with herself during the night and won. From now on she lived her own life and kept her deeper emotions firmly under lock and key. Nothing was ever going to hurt her again, because she was never going to become involved again. As for Blake—well, good riddance! He had brought her little but anguish.

That resolve still held when she opened the door to him next day. She could even view him with a total detachment, noting the lines of strain about eyes and mouth. He had suffered too, there was no doubt, but at least his agony was over. Whether he and Janine would stay together did not concern her. Nothing about him concerned her. She was free at last.

The solicitor was a man in his mid-fifties, obviously well versed in the art of dealing with couples who had little to say to each other.

'Let me see now,' he said when, preliminary introductions over, he had them seated side by side before him at the littered desk. 'You've been married how long?'

Donna answered for them both. 'It will be three years in mid-November.'

'Ah!' Greying brows drew together in a sudden frown. He studied the two of them in silence for a moment before saying briskly, 'I'm afraid that creates a certain difficulty. You see, a marriage has to have been in effect for a full three years before any petition for divorce can be considered.'

Once again it was Donna who responded; Blake seemed to be paying little attention to anything outside of his own thoughts. 'I . . . We didn't realise that.'

'Too few do.' The lawyer's tone was dry. 'Divorce has been made easier in latter years, but that particular rule still applies. The only exceptions would be in the case of extreme circumstances, such as actual physical abuse of a severe nature. I take it those grounds don't apply?'

'No.' Donna kept her gaze fixed on the thin, sharp-featured face, wishing Blake would say something—*any*thing. 'No, they don't. We just want a simple civilised decree.'

'An amicable parting of disillusioned parties?' The shrug held resignation. 'Mine not to reason why. Uncontested, I can have a decree nisi through in four weeks, the absolute six weeks after that. That will bring you to the end of January—the best I can offer.'

'Thanks.' Blake was on his feet, expression controlled. 'We'll call on you again in November. Donna?'

She accompanied him from the office feeling strangely detached from reality. Outside on the stairs she said helplessly, 'So much for that!'

'Two months isn't too long to wait, is it?' asked Blake with some sarcasm, descending ahead of her. 'We're both of us caught in the same trap.'

'With compensations for some, surely?' she retorted on a silky note. 'Janine will help you pass the time.'

He stopped dead in his tracks, turning on the narrow stairs to confront her with face gone savage. 'Leave Janine out of it!'

Donna stood her ground two steps above him, eyes blazing blue against the swift pallor of her skin. 'Why should I? You didn't. But then who could expect it? What I couldn't do for you she could. Be thankful for small mercies!'

'You little . . .'

He broke off suddenly, one hand going up to clasp his forehead, face whitening. Donna saw him start to sway and made a terrified, desperate grab for his sleeve, holding him against the pull of his slowly collapsing weight until he was safely down, if not too secure on the slope of the stairs. Her cry brought people running from both floors to find her cradling the beloved dark head in her arms as she tried to keep him from slipping down the rest of the flight.

'Call an ambulance!' she cried. 'My husband is ill!'

After that things happened swiftly. Blake was still unconscious when they wheeled him away from her at the hospital. She waited what seemed like an interminable time until a white-coated figure approached.

'Your husband appears to have formed a clot causing pressure on the brain,' the doctor informed her with creditable directness. 'We've sent him straight on up to surgery now. If you'd like to stay, there's a waiting room on the third floor. I'll get someone to bring you some coffee.'

If she'd like to stay! Wild horses wouldn't have dragged her away. The waiting room was comfortably furnished with soft deep chairs and a colour TV. Donna sat down and stared at the blank screen, her mind only just beginning to emerge from the numbing effect of shock. It was history repeating itself, she thought. Only this time the outcome might well be worse.

The telephone on the far wall drew her attention. They would be expecting him back at the museum by now. She should let them know.

Clive Needham answered the call, his concern immediate and genuine. Donna promised to call again the moment she had any further news, and settled down again to the long wait.

She was drinking a second cup of coffee procured by a considerate nurse when Janine arrived.

'Clive gave me the news,' she said. 'I felt I had to come.'

Donna looked at her without flinching, mentally contrasting the smoothly immaculate figure with her own dishevelled appearance and caring not a whit. 'Do you love him?' she demanded, and saw the grey-green eyes change expression.

'I don't think I need answer that. Not to you, at any rate.'

'Yes, you do.' The words came out clipped and

determined. 'If you love him you'll be prepared to accept him any way he comes out of this. Are you?'

Uncertainty flickered across the other woman's face. 'What are you trying to tell me? Has anyone mentioned the possibility of brain damage?'

'No,' Donna admitted. 'But it's there, isn't it? And I still want to know.'

'We'll wait and see, shall we?' Janine was in control again. 'Whatever happens you'll hardly need to be concerned.'

The smile was faint and humourless. 'Whatever happens I'll always be concerned. You see, *I* do love him. What's more, I'm going to fight for him.'

For once even Janine appeared to have no ready answer. She sat contemplating her entwined fingers with an odd expression for several moments before finally bringing herself to speak.

'You know, I never had much time for you at the best, but I have to give you credit for perseverance. Doesn't the fact that he walked out on you a couple of nights back make any difference?'

'Nothing makes any difference,' Donna returned evenly, 'so don't bother telling me where and how he spent those two nights.'

The blonde head came up slowly, eyes revealing a certain surprise. 'You think he was with me?'

'I *know* he was.' Donna watched the other woman's face, her breath catching suddenly and painfully in her throat. 'At least . . .'

The words came with reluctance as if drawn out against the will. 'The closest I've been to Blake this time round is what you saw for yourself the other night. Not for want of trying on my part, I'll admit, but he wasn't ready to play before then.'

Donna stared at her, trying to read the mind behind the too familiar features. 'He didn't come home for over an hour after I caught the two of you together.'

'Not my doing, I assure you. He left me standing.' Janine's tone was rueful. 'If it's any consolation, I've been feeling more than a little deflated myself this last couple of days. He's a rare kind of man.'

'He may be another kind of man when he wakens up,' Donna rejoined softly, refusing to acknowledge the word 'if'. 'Could you take that?'

The reply was immediate and honest. 'No, I couldn't. The man I want is the man I knew eighteen months ago.' She waited a brief moment then came to her feet, smoothing down her skirt with decisive fingers. 'I'd better be getting back. Keep us advised.'

Donna let her reach the door before saying her name, summoning a smile as she turned her head. 'Thanks.'

'No skin off my nose,' came the wry response. 'I'd lost anyway. I hope you have better luck.'

She needed more than luck, reflected Donna achingly as the door closed. She needed another miracle.

Time passed slowly. Occasionally a nurse or some other uniformed figure looked in, but they didn't linger. When the moment finally came she was ready for the worst, and could scarcely take in the detail. Blake had come through the operation successfully with no apparent signs of damage, the surgeon told her, although the latter assessment could only be verified on his recovery from anaesthetic, which would not be for another hour or so yet. If she wished to sit with him in the meantime she was free to do so.

They had put him in a private room on this same floor. Seeing him lying there with the plasma drip running into him took her back over the months as if they had never been. No lies this time, she promised herself, watching the unresponsive face. No false pride either. She would make him believe in her again if it was the last thing she ever did.

He started to come round in easy stages, opening his eyes almost exactly on the stated hour to lie looking blankly at the ceiling. Donna said his name softly, seeing intelligence dawn with heart-stopping relief and gratitude. She steeled herself to meet the gaze he turned in her direction.

'You're in hospital again,' she said. 'Only this time it's in England.'

'I know where I am.' He sounded surprisingly rational. 'I remember the pain starting when we were in that office having sentence declared, and feeling you grab me when I started to black out on the stairs.' The pause held a slow-growing awareness, the grey eyes never leaving her face. 'I remember everything. Our marriage, the separation, Incanta—the lot. It's a bit hazy round the edges, but the essence is there.'

'I'm glad.' Donna found it difficult to think straight. She tried to smile. 'That should make your work easier if nothing else. You had a lot to catch up on in those missing years.'

'It isn't work I'm thinking of,' he said. 'It's us. We've been married twice.'

'And both of them failures.' She shook her head to the look in his eyes. 'You know it's true, Blake. You couldn't make love to me because deep down you didn't want to make love to me. Janine proved who was the real root of the problem.'

'Janine proved nothing,' he declared on a wry note. 'Except that I was desperate enough to try anything. The affair we had was over a long time ago. I never had any yen to renew it.'

She said slowly, 'But you said the other night . . .'

'I know what I said the other night. I needed an excuse to get away. Making out it was only you who left me cold salvaged my pride to a certain degree.

Away from you I thought I might be able to work it out of my system.'

'And now?' She had to force the words. 'Is it still the same?'

The shrug was more sensed than seen. 'How would I know? I'm full of anaesthetic and my head aches like hell!' He paused again, momentarily closing his eyes. 'I have a whole lot of thinking to do, Donna. Just give me time.'

'As much as you want.' She rose unsteadily to her feet, making no attempt to kiss him or touch him in any way. 'Do you want me to come back tomorrow?'

The hesitation was brief. 'It might be best if you left it until I've got myself together again. The memory's back, but I'm still disoriented.'

'All right.' It was all she could do to keep her tone level. 'I'll phone. Perhaps you'd get the staff to pass on the message when you feel up to it.'

'Loud and clear.' His smile held irony. 'Just don't expect too much.'

She wanted to tell him then that she would settle for anything he could offer, but it wasn't the time. She had a desolate feeling that it never was going to be the time.

She went through the following days like an automaton, living only for the moments when she phoned the hospital for the daily progress report. Dr Mitchell was making an excellent recovery, she was told on each occasion with some formality, causing her to wonder just what reason Blake had given the staff for her non-appearance at his bedside. Not the truth, for certain.

She made herself go out during the day, even if only to wander through the stores or join the tourists in their endless parade along the city streets. The evenings were the worst, although she resolutely refused to sit drooping over her thoughts, and spent the hours improving her knowledge with the help of Blake's books. If the time came when she had to start looking for a job again, she intended to be prepared. A career could be a substitute for marriage if one wanted it to be. Edith Remington had found her own kind of fulfilment in her work.

The eventual call from the hospital to say that Dr Mitchell was ready to be discharged left her in something of a dilemma, as it gave her no hint of his attitude. Someone, however, had to take in his clothes and he could hardly go straight from hospital to a hotel. Playing it by ear was the only recourse she had.

Blake was sitting talking with one of the nurses when she got there. The latter gave her a frozen glance in passing, her meaning only too clear.

'She thinks I've been deliberately neglecting you,' Donna said ruefully as she opened the suitcase she had brought with her. 'That's hardly fair.'

'Does it matter what anyone else thinks?' Blake responded without inflection, watching the movement of her hands. 'How do you feel about my coming back to the flat?'

'Where else would you go?' She pushed back the heavy hair from her face in a purely nervous gesture. 'The sofa is big enough to use as a bed.'

'So it is.' It was impossible to tell what he might be thinking. The grey eyes were totally unreadable. 'You brought the car?'

She nodded, unable to speak for the moment. With the suitcase emptied of its load, she snapped the locks and straightened. 'I'll wait for you outside. Do you have to see anyone before we leave?'

'It's all been taken care of,' he said. 'They want me back for a check-up in a month, but apart from that it's all plain sailing.'

Hardly that, she reflected. Too much lay between

them. She left him to dress.

Lunch was a first priority by the time they reached the flat. Donna had prepared most of the meal before leaving; now all she had to do was reheat the soup and put the pizzas under a hot grill. They were sitting over coffee when she finally reached the end of her tether, putting down her cup into the saucer with a hand that shook.

'Blake, *talk* to me!' she appealed. 'We can hardly go on just ignoring the whole situation.'

'I didn't intend to ignore it,' he said. 'I was simply waiting for the right moment.'

'To tell me what?'

'Not a lot.' The shrug made light of the words. 'I've had a couple of long chats with the head shrink and learned a few things about myself I'd as soon not have known. Apart from that the situation remains, as you might say, at status quo.' His mouth twisted. 'Understanding motivation is only half the battle, apparently. The spirit doth not the flesh command.'

So nothing had changed. She should have known. What he had learned to do, she gathered, was live with the fact. In some ways acceptance was the worst part of it.

'I'm listening,' she said softly. 'Please, Blake. I'd like to understand too.'

It took him a long time to begin. When he did it was with his eyes on his cup as he used the spoon to stir the rapidly cooling liquid. 'That blow on the head was only partially to blame for the memory loss,' he said. 'Pressure on certain parts of the brain can affect memory, it seems, but it would probably be more of a blurring than a total blacking out. What happens is that the emotions seize on the excuse to cancel out what they don't want to remember. Hence the return to our wedding day when it was all new and the mistakes were still to come.'

'A fresh start,' she murmured. 'That's how I felt too.'

His head came up then, eyes steady on her face. 'Donna, you're no fool now and you were no fool then. How can I be expected to believe you really imagined we could start afresh?'

'I told you—shock. And desperation. If you remember the night you came after me at Incanta you'll know why I was desperate.' She was putting everything into convincing him, her voice trembling with the effort. 'If I didn't love you before I loved you by then. Enough to make me irrational when it came to a swift decision.'

There was a certain rueful quality in his expression. 'I remember the night in the cave, and what I said to you next morning. That was cruel, I have to admit.'

'It was understandable.' She let the pause lie for a moment or two before adding gently, 'That's not all of it. You lived with me without trusting me for three months, yet it didn't stop you making love to me. Why should it happen so suddenly after all that time?'

'According to advice, I was making a last ditch stand.' His tone held irony. 'Forcing the issue, I believe it's called. If my hold on you was purely sexual then the lack of it would prove just how shallow the relationship between us was.'

'Only I didn't go,' said Donna. 'You did. Doesn't that prove anything?'

He smiled faintly. 'It proves I couldn't take my own medicine any more. You weren't exactly loth to discuss a divorce.'

'I had my pride too,' she pointed out. 'At that time I was convinced you wanted Janine back.' She stopped there, shaking her head in resigned acknowledgment. 'You know, we could go on talking round it for ever and never find an adequate solution. I can't *prove* my feelings for you, Blake. I can only show you.'

The cynicism was still there in his eyes. 'How?'

'Like this.' She got up and went to him, pushing aside the coffee table with her knee to bend down and put her lips to the taped dressing covering the right side of his forehead, her hands resting lightly on his shoulders. When he still made no move she lowered herself to knee level so she could see his face, injecting every atom of feeling she could conjure into her voice. 'Blake, I'm not going to pretend that it means nothing to me if you never make total physical love to me again. I'd be a liar if I tried. But I can live with it. I can live with anything but losing you again.'

His expression revealed little. 'Time will tell,' he said. 'But I'll try to believe that.'

She had the sense not to push for anything more. Time was one thing they had plenty of.

The day went through its phases, lengthy but not dull. They talked about the museum, of the success of the exhibition. Janine had already gone on to Birmingham to prepare the way for the transfer. Donna was aware that the archaeologist still planned on persuading Blake to join forces on a second expedition some time in the not too far distant future, but refrained from mentioning the fact. Saving their marriage was more important than any expedition—to her if to no one else. She had nothing to spare for petty jealousies and resentments

Bedtime brought a measure of uncertainty, quickly relieved by Blake's calm announcement that he would be sleeping on the sofa. For the time being it was probably for the best, Donna told herself, although the day would come, she hoped, when he could bring himself to at least bear to be near her again.

They said goodnight like brother and sister after she had brought through the bedding from the linen cupboard. With two doors closed between them, Donna lay in the centre of the double bed and with difficulty controlled the urge to go back to him. Patience and forbearance had to be her strong suits. She could only wish she had practised either or both a little harder in the past.

Sleep overcame her eventually, despite her endlessly revolving thoughts. In her dreams she was back at Incanta, reliving the earthquake all over again, seeing the falling stones burying Blake beneath them, only this time unable to move because she too was trapped by some great weight. Then the scene changed and it was Blake himself who was pinning her down, his lips seeking her breasts, her throat and finally her mouth; only it was no longer a dream, because she was awake and already responding, holding the strong, smoothly muscled body to her in a fury of sensation, moving beneath him with a wildness that took them both over the brink at the same ecstatic instant to leave them spent and mindless in the vacuum beyond.

It was Blake who broke the spell by starting to laugh, his whole body shaking with it. 'Oh, God,' he gasped, 'you can't know what that felt like!'

'I do. Oh, I do!' Donna was laughing too, the joy and relief pealing from her. 'Blake, I love you. I really love you!'

'I know. I love you too.' He sobered enough to kiss her, his lips so tender she could scarcely believe their message. 'I've been in a dark place, my darling, but it's over. It's finally over!'

'How?' she asked, kissing him back. 'Why, Blake? What . . .'

'I woke up and I wanted you—just like that. I couldn't even wait for you to wake up properly. Not that it made any difference. Asleep or awake, you're the best lay any man could have!'

'Hey!' she protested in mock indignation, matching his mood. 'I'll have you know I do not come on that way for any Tom, Dick or Harry!' Her tone softened, her hands resting each side of the lean face. 'And never did.'

'I know that too. Now.' Blake's expression was difficult to gauge. 'The best I can do is to say there has never been and never will be anyone else to equal you—not in any sense. We have a lot of lost time to catch up on, Donna. Where do we start?'

Her smile came slow and inviting. 'Right here and now,' she whispered.

Harlequin Plus

A WORD ABOUT THE AUTHOR

Sometimes Kay Thorpe finds she has become two different people: the writer, at her happiest when involved in the world of books and authors; and the housewife, turning her hand to the everyday needs of husband and son. Once in a while, she finds it difficult to step from one role to the other. She likes cooking, for instance, but she finds it can be an irritating interruption when she's preoccupied with work on a novel, so the quality of her efforts in the kitchen tends to be a little erratic. She says, "As my husband once remarked, my writing gives life a fascinating element of uncertainty: one day a perfect coq au vin, the next a couple of burned chops!"

Luckily Kay has daily professional help with her housework, and that leaves her time to indulge in her hobbies. Like many other Harlequin authors, she admits to being a voracious consumer of books, a quality she shares with her readers. She likes music and horseback riding, which she does in the countryside near her home. But her favorite hobby is travel—especially to places that will make good settings for her books.